MUSE SAGA

VOL. 1

MR. BROGATH

NEWSLETTER

Want to stay up to date on everything I'm doing, and be the first to know about new releases?

Join my mailing list:
mrbrogath.com/newsletter

You'll get some cool exclusive content too!

ACKNOWLEDGMENTS

To my awesome patrons over on Patreon. Without you, that whole starving artist thing would become a bit too literal.

Thank you.

Dear Reader,

It is with some trepidation that I tell you the tales you are about to read. As you will soon realize, my memory is far from perfect. There are gaps and holes that I struggle to fill, moments that remain shrouded in fog. I do my best to recall the important details, the people I have met and the struggles we have faced together.

The truth is, many of these particular stories have become blurred over time. I may have added certain flourishes here and there for the sake of drama. You must forgive any minor discrepancies or exaggerations. After all, what author does not take some liberties with the facts when crafting a tale? I wish only to communicate the spirit of my many adventures - the friendships, the reflections, and the endless surprises that await around each bend in the road.

As a raccoon without my memories, I find my story constantly being rewritten. Like these pages themselves, my reality is something of a work in progress. Sometimes the embellishments bring me closer to the truth of who I really am, other times they lead me further astray. Yet pressing on, regardless of what paths are open before me, seems the only way forward. After all, that is the very nature of storytelling - and living.

So stay tuned, dear reader. Our tale together continues. Even now, new adventures await, new mysteries cry out for answers, and old friends beckon me closer to home. I can only promise to share what I find - memories intact, fragmented or perhaps completely fictionalized - and hope that you remain by my side as I venture ever onward into the unknown.

Your humble narrator and companion on this journey,
   Mr. Brogath

CHAPTER ONE

Mr. Brogath awoke with a start, surrounded by the musty scent of damp earth. He blinked his beady eyes and looked around in confusion. His small raccoon paws sunk into the soft, moss-covered ground as he tried to stand up.

"Where...?" he muttered, his voice barely audible even to himself. Mr. Brogath stood in the middle of the dense forest, his small frame illuminated by a patch of sunlight that had managed to peep through the foliage. He surveyed what lay before him with awe and wonderment. The trees were tall and their trunks ancient and gnarled, reaching up into the sky like bony fingers. Their branches were inter-twined, forming a protective canopy above him while thick vines formed a web-like backdrop all around him. It was both mesmerizing and disorienting, as if he had stumbled upon some kind of mysterious labyrinth.

No matter how far he travelled, it seemed like there was no end in sight. Mr Brogath let out a sigh and set off on his journey through this strange new world that he had stum-bled upon. He hoped that eventually he would find his way back home - wherever that may be...

He continued to walk, taking in the sights and sounds of this strange place. There were birds chirping in the distance and small animals scurrying about on the forest floor. It was amazing how peaceful it felt here, as if the forest itself was alive and breathing.

"Who am I?" Mr. Brogath thought, his mind spinning. He shook his head, trying to clear away the fog that clouded his memory. For now, he was simply a raccoon – an ordinary creature in an extraordinary world.

As Mr. Brogath ventured deeper into the forest, he became aware of its unique features. The flora was unlike anything he had ever seen – if, indeed, he had ever seen anything at all. Luminous mushrooms basked in their own eerie glow, and plants sprouted from the ground with leaves shaped like stars. The mushrooms smelled delicious, like a freshly baked pie, and he didn't see the harm in having a bite or two. Or three.

As his head began to buzz from the unanticipated effects of the mushrooms, the forest took on a new and exaggerated vividness.

The air was thick with the fragrance of exotic flowers, some of which emitted musical notes when touched.

"Ah!" Mr. Brogath gasped, jumping back as a flower snapped shut, narrowly missing his curious paw. "Feisty little thing, aren't you?"

"Thought you'd never ask," replied the flower, its petals quivering with delight. Mr. Brogath stared, dumbfounded. He couldn't remember the last time a plant had spoken to him – or if such a thing had ever occurred at all.

"Can all flowers... talk?" he asked hesitantly.

"Only the charming ones," the flower retorted, striking what Mr. Brogath assumed to be a pose.

"Charming, indeed," he murmured, unable to resist a

smile. He continued onward, marveling at the unusual fauna that accompanied the flora. Creatures with iridescent feathers flitted through the canopy, while insects the size of his paw scurried underfoot.

"Are you lost?" a sultry voice asked. Mr. Brogath looked up to see a snake draped over a branch, its scales shimmering like liquid silver.

"Lost? I can't be certain," he replied, scratching his head. "I don't... remember where I'm supposed to be."

"Ah, memory loss," the snake sighed, flicking its tongue. "That's always a tough one. Well, good luck on your journey, little raccoon."

"Thank you," Mr. Brogath said, nodding his appreciation before continuing on his way. The world around him was strange and disorienting, but it held a certain charm – if only he could figure out who he was and why he was here.

"Maybe this is all just a dream," he mused as he crossed paths with a beetle wearing a monocle. "Or perhaps I've gone mad."

"Either way," the beetle replied, adjusting its eyepiece, "it's quite the adventure, isn't it?"

"Indeed," agreed Mr. Brogath, feeling a spark of excitement despite the lingering confusion. "Quite the adventure, indeed."

The forest gave way to a small village, its cobblestone streets lined with cottages that appeared to have sprouted directly from the ground. Their walls were woven from vines and branches, their roofs made of thick leaves that provided ample shade. The villagers moved about their day as if they hadn't noticed Mr. Brogath. He wondered whether they simply didn't see him or if raccoons were an ordinary sight around these parts.

"Hello there," Mr. Brogath said to a passing woman,

attempting to engage her in conversation. She glanced at him with wide eyes before hurrying away, clutching her basket of vegetables tighter.

"Ah, well," he muttered, feeling a pang of frustration. "At least she didn't scream."

As he wandered further into the village, he began to notice more peculiarities. The people here wore clothing fashioned from flowers and leaves, their hair adorned with delicate blossoms. Laughter echoed through the air as children chased after large, bumbling bees with wings like stained glass.

"Excuse me, sir," Mr. Brogath said to a man carrying a load of firewood. "Would you mind telling me where I am?"

"Rabid raccoon!" the man exclaimed, dropping his bundle in surprise. "And... it can talk!"

"Indeed, I can," Mr. Brogath replied with a touch of annoyance. "But I'm afraid I don't remember much else. Perhaps you can help me?"

The man eyed him warily before shaking his head. "I don't know what kind of trickery this is, but I want no part in it." With that, he hurriedly gathered his firewood and left Mr. Brogath standing alone.

"Such hospitality," Mr. Brogath grumbled under his breath. He was beginning to grow disheartened when a young girl approached him, her eyes filled with curiosity rather than fear.

"Are you lost, Mr. Raccoon?" she asked, tilting her head.

"Mr. Brogath, actually," he corrected, a small smile tugging at his lips. "And yes, I suppose I am."

"My name is Lily," the girl said, extending a hand to pet him gently. "You don't look like a bad raccoon. Just a bit odd... Oh, and you're foaming at the mouth a bit."

"Odd" seemed to be an understatement, considering his

current circumstances, but Mr. Brogath decided not to comment on that. "Thank you for your kindness, Lily. Everyone else seems rather... frightened of me," he said, wiping the froth from his lips.

"Maybe they're just not used to talking raccoons," she suggested with a shrug. "I think it's exciting. Like a storybook come to life. There's magic in these lands, but it's so rare I was beginning to think it was only stories."

"In a land where so many plants and animals talk, that seems odd," Mr. Brogath said. "I hope the mushroom I ate wasn't able to talk..."

"Oh no. Did you eat one of the glowing mushrooms in the forest?"

"Am I going to die?" he asked, panicked.

She giggled. "No, you're not going to die, but that explains the foaming. Just don't believe everything you see and hear for the rest of the day... Especially if that thing you're seeing or hearing doesn't normally talk. Those mushrooms aren't dangerous, but you better stay put while the effects wear off."

"Ah, well, perhaps you can help me, then?" Mr. Brogath ventured. "I seem to have lost my memory, and I'm trying to find out who I am and where I belong."

Lily hesitated for a moment, biting her lip as she weighed the decision. Finally, she nodded. "Alright. You can stay with me and my family for now. We'll figure this out together."

"Thank you, Lily," he said earnestly, touched by her offer. "Your kindness is truly appreciated."

"Come on, then," she beckoned, leading him towards her home. "Let's get you settled in before we start asking questions."

As they walked side by side, Mr. Brogath couldn't help

but feel a sense of hope blooming within him. Perhaps, with Lily's help, he would finally begin to unravel the mystery of his identity and find his place in this strange, enchanting world.

Once they reached Lily's modest home, Mr. Brogath was introduced to her family, who were understandably cautious but warmed up to him quickly as he expressed his gratitude and shared his plight. At dinner, Lily served a steaming bowl of some sort of stew, full of unfamiliar vegetables and chunks of tender meat. Lily's mother had dumped in some powder she said would help with the mushroom's hallucinogenic effects.

"Is this...?" Mr. Brogath hesitated, sniffing at the steam rising from the bowl.

"Goat stew," Lily said with a grin. "Don't worry, I made sure there are no raccoons in it."

"Ah, well, that's reassuring," he replied, chuckling nervously. He took a tentative bite and was pleasantly surprised by the rich, hearty flavors. "This is delicious!" he exclaimed between mouthfuls.

"Thank you," Lily beamed. "My mother taught me how to cook."

As they ate, Mr. Brogath listened intently to the conversations around the table, eager to learn more about the kingdom and its people. The topics ranged from local gossip to news of distant lands, giving him a glimpse into the daily lives of the villagers.

"Everyone seems to know everyone else here," he observed.

"Small villages like ours tend to be that way," Lily explained. "But we're just a tiny part of the kingdom. There are cities where people don't even know their neighbors. We're on the very outskirts, so fortunately we're not often involved in the kingdom's squabbles and rarely noticed by King Elgron."

"Remarkable," Mr. Brogath mused, his curiosity piqued.

Over the next few days, Mr. Brogath accompanied Lily as she went about her tasks, meeting the villagers and exploring the surrounding area. Despite the initial shock and apprehension towards his appearance, many of the villagers soon grew fond of the talking raccoon, finding his earnest charm and quick wit endearing.

"Mr. Brogath, meet Old Man Jenkins," Lily said one day as they approached a wizened figure tending to a vegetable garden.

"Ah, so you're the talking raccoon everyone's been going on about," Old Man Jenkins said gruffly but with a twinkle in his eye. "You've got half the village in an uproar and the other half thinking we've all gone mad."

"Apologies for the inconvenience, sir," Mr. Brogath replied, dipping his head in a gesture of respect. "I assure you, I am quite harmless."

"Ha! You remind me of a traveling bard who came through here once, spinning fantastic tales and enchanting us with his songs." Old Man Jenkins cackled, clearly amused by the comparison.

"An interesting parallel," Mr. Brogath mused, wondering if there might be some truth to it.

Mr. Brogath continued to adapt to the village life, learning more about its customs and history from Lily and her family. He discovered that laughter often disarmed even the most skeptical individuals, and he used this to his advantage as he interacted with the villagers. And as he learned more about their lives and hardships, he couldn't help but feel a growing sense of attachment to these people and their world.

"Thank you, Lily," he whispered to her one evening as they sat together under the stars. "For everything."

"Of course," she replied softly, smiling at him. "We're friends, aren't we? And friends help each other out."

"Indeed, they do," Mr. Brogath agreed, gazing up at the night sky. "I may not know where I come from, but I'm starting to feel welcome here, thanks to you and your kindness."

"Maybe that's what matters most," Lily said thoughtfully. "That you found a place where you feel welcome and at home."

"Perhaps," Mr. Brogath murmured, lost in thought. There was still so much he didn't know or understand, but the journey of self-discovery had become less daunting with Lily by his side. And as they sat there together, bathed in starlight, a small but persistent voice in the back of his mind whispered that maybe, just maybe, this was where he was meant to be all along.

In the days that followed, Mr. Brogath became increasingly fascinated by the unique features of this magical world. As he and Lily strolled through the village, he couldn't help but marvel at the architecture. The houses, made of a peculiar blend of stone and wood, were adorned with intricate carvings that seemed to tell stories of heroes and mythical creatures.

"I've been meaning to ask you about this," Mr. Brogath exclaimed, running his fingers over one of the carvings on a nearby house. "The craftsmanship is extraordinary! Is there a meaning behind these symbols?"

Lily smiled knowingly. "Each carving tells a story from

our history or a lesson we wish to pass down to future generations. It's our way of preserving knowledge without relying on written texts."

"Interesting," Mr. Brogath murmured, his curiosity piqued.

As they continued their walk, they came upon a group of villagers engaged in an odd dance. Their movements were fluid and synchronized, accompanied by the rhythmic beating of drums. Mr. Brogath watched, transfixed, as the dancers swirled around each other like leaves caught in a whirlwind.

"What are they doing?" he asked Lily, his eyes never leaving the mesmerizing scene.

"It's a traditional dance to honor the spirits of the forest," she explained. "We believe that performing it brings good fortune and protection to our village. Maybe you're a forest spirit!"

Mr. Brogath smiled and nodded thoughtfully, taking mental notes as he observed the customs of this new world. He was determined to understand every aspect of it, even if some parts seemed strange or puzzling to him.

However, his memory loss often left him feeling disoriented and frustrated. There were times when he struggled to comprehend the simplest tasks, like tying knots or understanding the local currency. His inability to remember his past, combined with the peculiarities of this world, made for a challenging existence.

"Here, let me help you," Lily offered one day as she noticed him fumbling with the laces of a child's shoe he was trying to help. Her fingers deftly secured the knots, and Mr. Brogath sighed in relief.

"Thank you," he said, grateful for her patience and

understanding. "I don't know why I can't seem to grasp even the most basic things sometimes."

Lily looked at him sympathetically. "It's not your fault," she reassured him. "You're learning an entirely new way of life, and that's bound to be difficult. But you're adapting remarkably well, all things considered."

Mr. Brogath gave her a weak smile. "I suppose so," he conceded. "But it's still incredibly frustrating."

"Give yourself time," Lily advised. "I'm sure it will get easier as you become more familiar with our customs and way of life."

"Perhaps," Mr. Brogath murmured, unconvinced. But deep down, a part of him longed to believe her words, even as another part feared that he would never truly belong in this strange new world.

Despite these challenges, Mr. Brogath continued to explore and learn. And though the path before him was fraught with uncertainty, he couldn't deny the thrill of discovery that coursed through him with every new revelation.

"Sometimes I wonder if I'll ever regain my memories," he confessed to Lily one evening as they sat on the edge of the village square, watching the sun set over the forest.

"Maybe you will," she replied gently. "And maybe you won't. But either way, you're creating new memories here, with us. And isn't that just as important?"

Mr. Brogath considered her words, his gaze lingering on the vibrant colors that painted the sky. And as he looked out over the village that had welcomed him so warmly, he couldn't help but think that perhaps she was right.

"Can you explain why everyone was wearing those colorful hats today?" he asked.

"Of course," Lily replied, adjusting her own hat with a

smile. "Today was the Festival of the Sunflower. It's a celebration of the harvest, and the hats represent the sunflowers that have grown in abundance this year."

"Ah, I see," Mr. Brogath nodded, marveling at the intricacies of their customs. "So that's why we picked so many earlier."

As time went on, Lily continued to help Mr. Brogath overcome his challenges, teaching him about the village's history, its legends, and even the local cuisine.

"Try this," she offered one day, handing him a steaming bowl filled with an assortment of colorful vegetables and chunks of meat.

"What is it?" he asked, sniffing cautiously.

"Another kind of stew," she explained. "It's a traditional dish we prepare during the colder months. It's made with fresh ingredients from the forest."

"Delicious," Mr. Brogath declared after taking a careful bite. "I might even prefer this to the nuts and berries I used to eat."

"Really?" Lily laughed, visibly pleased by his enthusiasm. "Well, there's plenty more where that came from."

"Thank you, Lily," Mr. Brogath said gratefully, looking around at the village that had become his home. "For everything."

"Of course, Mr. Brogath," she replied warmly. "We're all here to help each other. Come on, let's go explore the forest again. I think you'll like what I have to show you today," Lily said.

Together, they ventured into the woods, where strange flora and fauna seemed to sprout from every crevice. With each step, Mr. Brogath marveled at the fantastical creatures that darted between the shadows – birds with iridescent plumage, insects with jeweled wings, and moss-covered beasts that lumbered lazily among the trees.

"Is that a... floating flower?" Mr. Brogath asked in astonishment, pointing at a delicate blossom suspended in midair by an invisible thread.

"Those are wind lilies," Lily explained, plucking one from the air and handing it to him gently. "They drift on the breeze and spread their seeds far and wide."

"Amazing," he whispered, watching the petals dance in the dappled sunlight.

"Everything here is amazing," she said softly, her eyes filled with wonder. "And each time we explore, we find something new and exciting. It's a lot more fun showing someone something they've never seen before."

"Indeed," he agreed, his heart swelling with gratitude for the opportunity to experience it all.

But as much as he reveled in these discoveries, Mr. Brogath couldn't shake a nagging sense of unease that settled in the back of his mind. The question of his memory loss – and why he seemed so uninterested in regaining it – gnawed at him like a persistent itch.

"Are you okay, Mr. Brogath?" Lily asked, her brow furrowed with concern.

"Of course," he assured her with a smile, not wanting to dampen her spirits. "Just lost in thought, that's all."

"About your past?"

"You got me," he admitted hesitantly. "But I don't want to dwell on it right now. There's so much to see, and I don't want to miss any of it."

"Alright," she said, accepting his answer. "But if you ever want to talk about it, I'm here for you."

"Thank you, Lily," he murmured, touched by her unwavering support. "I truly appreciate that."

Mr. Brogath couldn't help but feel a deep sense of wonder and excitement despite his lingering questions. The village, the forest, and the people within them had become his home, and he was determined to live every moment to its fullest.

Yet, in the back of his mind, the mystery of his memory loss remained — a puzzle waiting to be solved and a clue to the larger story unfolding around him. For now, however, Mr. Brogath chose to focus on the present, embracing the life he had stumbled upon and the friendships that had blossomed along the way. But as time went on, he would soon discover that the answers he sought were far more intricate and complex than he could have ever imagined.

CHAPTER TWO

One evening, Mr. Brogath decided he would take it upon himself to gather some herbs for one of Lily's excellent stews. Nocturnal eyes had that advantage, of course. Even returning late, he would have no problem finding his way. Distracted by another village in the far distance he wasn't familiar with, he strayed further and further from his intended path.

The sun dipped low in the sky, casting long shadows across the quaint village. Mr. Brogath, a raccoon with an air of curiosity about him, scampered along the outskirts of the village, his nose twitching as he took in the unfamiliar scents. He couldn't shake the feeling that there was something more to his existence than simply being a raccoon, but try as he might, he couldn't remember anything beyond the past few weeks.

With a sigh, Mr. Brogath continued on his errand. As he padded along, he couldn't help but notice that the village seemed strangely quiet, as though its inhabitants were holding their breath in anticipation of something.

"Odd," thought Mr. Brogath, his brow furrowing

beneath his mask-like markings. "It feels like everyone is hiding from something. But what could be so frightening in such a peaceful place?"

As he ambled along the rocky path, Mr. Brogath noticed a well-worn road leading off into the distance that passed through the village. Drawn by curiosity, he decided to investigate further. The village wasn't just quiet. It was empty.

But before he could make it through the village, he heard the sound of marching hooves. He turned around and saw two soldiers on horseback coming his way. Instinctively, he attempted to find a place to hide, but it was too late. The guards had already spotted him and were ordering him to stop.

"Wait! I was just exploring!" Mr. Brogath pleaded, trying to explain his actions before they had a chance to react. But his words fell on deaf ears as the guards tightened their grip on their weapons and inched closer towards him.

"A magical creature!" one of them exclaimed, pointing their swords at Mr. Brogath while the other dismounted from his horse and began moving towards him. "King Elgron will want to know about this!"

It was clear that Mr. Brogath had mistakenly wandered onto forbidden territory and now faced imminent capture.

"Please, just listen to me," Mr. Brogath implored, his voice cracking with desperation. "I'm not a threat, I swear!"

But the guards paid him no heed, their eyes filled with suspicion and determination. As they closed in on the hapless raccoon, Mr. Brogath's heart pounded in his chest, his mind racing with questions about his true nature and the uncertain fate that awaited him.

Upon arriving at an enormous castle, the soldiers roughly seized Mr. Brogath by his furry limbs. Despite his frantic struggles, they quickly carried him through the winding corridors of the castle, the torchlit walls casting eerie shadows around them.

"Please, let me go!" Mr. Brogath cried, his little heart pounding. "I'm not a threat! I didn't mean to trespass!"

"Silence, beast!" one of the guards snapped, tightening his grip on the squirming raccoon.

As they entered a grand chamber, Mr. Brogath's eyes widened at the sight of King Elgron. The imposing figure sat on an ornate throne of gold and ebony, his icy eyes piercing into Mr. Brogath's very soul. The king's stern features were accentuated by a clean-shaven face, and his regal attire seemed to shimmer in the dim light.

"Your Majesty," a guard announced, bowing deeply, "we have captured this... creature."

King Elgron rose from the throne and approached Mr. Brogath, his gaze unrelenting. "So, you are a harbinger of ill fortune that has dared to enter my domain. Did one of the wizards enchant you?" His voice was as cold as the stone floor beneath him.

"Your Majesty, please!" Mr. Brogath stammered. "I don't even know what that means! My name is Mr. Brogath and I'm just a lost raccoon. I was picking herbs!"

"Raccoons do not speak, creature," the King said, his tone dripping with disdain. "You must be a spy."

"Believe me, sire, I am just as shocked by my ability to speak as you are!" Mr. Brogath protested, his voice trembling. "If I'm under an enchantment, I don't know anything about it!"

"Your lies will not save you," King Elgron declared. "I shall have the truth from you, one way or another."

As Mr. Brogath's mind raced with confusion and fear, he considered his options. He could continue to plead his innocence, but the King seemed utterly convinced of his guilt. Or he could try to weave a tale that might persuade the King to let him go.

"Alright, sire, if you must know the truth..." Mr. Brogath began hesitantly, his thoughts still scrambled as he tried to concoct a story on the spot.

"Speak!" King Elgron demanded, his eyes narrowing in suspicion.

"Your Majesty, I was once a human," Mr. Brogath said, his voice growing stronger as he spun his tale. "A powerful wizard transformed me into this raccoon form as punishment for... for stealing a prized amulet."

King Elgron leaned forward, his interest piqued by the mention of a powerful wizard. "And why would you steal this amulet?" he asked, his eyes narrowing.

"Because I was desperate, sire," Mr. Brogath replied, trying to sound as pitiful as possible. "I was starving, and I thought the amulet could be sold for food. You know these wizards and their expensive baubles. I was sure he'd never even miss it."

"Ha! A likely tale!" King Elgron scoffed, but before he could continue interrogating Mr. Brogath, a sudden explosion rocked the castle, causing both the raccoon and the king to jump in surprise.

"Your Majesty!" Commander Thorne burst into the room, panting heavily. "We're under attack! A wizard of immense power is laying waste to our defenses!"

"By the gods! This is your doing, isn't it, you wretched creature?" King Elgron bellowed, pointing an accusing finger at Mr. Brogath.

"Wha- no, Your Majesty!" Mr. Brogath stammered, his heart pounding with fear. "I have nothing to do with this!"

"Silence!" King Elgron ordered, turning to his commander. "Commander Thorne, take this cursed being to the dungeons. Find out about his ties to this treacherous wizard!"

"Your Majesty, are you certain interrogating him now is the best course of action? I can be of more use on the front lines," Commander Thorne said hesitantly, clearly torn between his loyalty to the king and his concern for the kingdom's safety.

"Are you questioning my orders, Commander?" King Elgron roared, his face turning an alarming shade of red.

"Of course not, sire," Commander Thorne replied quickly, bowing his head in submission. "I shall carry out your command at once."

"Please, Your Majesty, I swear to you that I have nothing to do with this attack!" Mr. Brogath pleaded as he was dragged away by the guards, his small heart hammering against his chest.

"Save your lies for the dungeon rats!" King Elgron spat, his gaze never leaving the raccoon's terrified eyes. "I will deal with you once this wizard has been vanquished!"

As Mr. Brogath was dragged deeper into the castle, he couldn't help but feel a sense of despair washing over him. He was innocent, yet the king would not listen to him. How could he prove his innocence? And how could he escape this grim fate that had befallen him?

"Think, Brogath, think," he whispered to himself, determined to find a way out of this mess. But as the cold stone walls of the dungeon closed around him, hope seemed to fade with each passing moment.

The cold, clammy walls of the dungeon seemed to close

in on Mr. Brogath as Commander Thorne roughly shoved him into his cell. The heavy door slammed shut behind him, echoing through the dark corridors like a death knell. The raccoon's heart raced as he tried to take in his surroundings; the floor was slick with dampness, and the smell of mold and despair pervaded the air.

"Don't get too comfortable," sneered Commander Thorne, peering through the bars at Mr. Brogath. "This won't take long."

"Please, sir," Mr. Brogath pleaded, despair evident in his voice, "I'm innocent! I know nothing of this wizard or his deeds!"

"King Elgron thinks you're involved somehow, and that's enough for me," replied Thorne coldly. "My orders are to extract any information you have about this wizard, and I intend to do just that."

Mr. Brogath shuddered at the thought of what this extraction of information might entail. He racked his brain for some memory or knowledge of the wizard but found only the void left by his amnesia. "I swear, I don't know anything!" he insisted, desperation creeping into his voice.

"Then I suggest you start remembering," said Thorne menacingly. "Mr. Brogath," he began, his voice cold and detached. "I'd like to believe that you're innocent in all of this, but the facts are difficult to ignore. You were caught just before the attack. Can you explain that? Are you saying it was all just a coincidence?"

Mr. Brogath took a deep breath and met the commander's gaze with as much determination as he could muster. "I was merely exploring, sir. I had no idea I was entering forbidden territory."

"Convenient," Thorne remarked dryly, his eyes narrowing. "And you expect me to believe that you have nothing to do with this wizard?"

"Absolutely!" Mr. Brogath exclaimed, a note of desperation creeping into his voice. "I swear, I've never even heard of such a person, let alone met or conspired with him. I'm simply a raccoon caught in the wrong place at the wrong time!"

Commander Thorne paced in front of the cell bars, his fingers tapping rhythmically against his thigh, a telltale sign of his skepticism. "Very well, let's say I believe you for now. Tell me more about yourself. What were you doing prior to wandering into our patrol?"

Mr. Brogath hesitated, his mind racing. He could tell Commander Thorne about Lily and her village so they could verify his story, but what if that put them in danger? "I... I don't know," he lied. "My memories are foggy. I can't remember anything before waking up in the woods near the destroyed village. When the patrol found me, I was looking for herbs."

"Amnesia, huh?" Thorne snorted. "How very convenient, again."

"Please, Commander," Mr. Brogath pleaded. "I understand why you're skeptical, but I truly know nothing about this wizard or his motives. I just want to find out who I am and why I'm here."

Thorne regarded Mr. Brogath with a long, searching look, weighing his words carefully. "Alright," he finally said. "I'll give you the benefit of the doubt for now. But if I find any evidence that links you to this attack, you can be sure that the king will show no mercy."

"Thank you, Commander," Mr. Brogath whispered, relief flooding through him, though it was tempered by an unsettling awareness of the precariousness of his situation.

"Let's start from the beginning," Thorne said, shifting gears into a more psychological mode of interrogation. "What do you remember about your life? Your family? Friends?"

Mr. Brogath racked his brain, trying to dredge up some fragment of memory, but all he found was a yawning chasm of emptiness before meeting Lily. "I... I don't remember anything," he said. It was mostly the truth, after all.

"Interesting," Thorne mused, tapping his chin thoughtfully. "It seems we're at an impasse, then. You claim innocence, yet you conveniently have no recollection of your past. You must understand why that makes us suspicious, Mr. Brogath."

"Of course," Mr. Brogath replied, his heart sinking as he realized the futility of his situation. No matter how earnestly he protested, the truth remained that he had no way of proving his innocence without endangering his friends – and with each passing moment, his chances of convincing Commander Thorne grew slimmer.

As the shadows continued to dance around them, Mr. Brogath couldn't help but feel that they mirrored his own darkening prospects. He understood that he needed to provide something, anything, to sway Commander Thorne's opinion. But what could he possibly offer when he had nothing but his own word to rely on?

Desperation clawed at Mr. Brogath's chest, tightening its grip like a vise. It was then that he had a sudden epiphany; if the truth could not save him, perhaps a lie would.

"Wait!" Mr. Brogath blurted out, his eyes widening with apparent revelation. "I do remember something now! The wizard... his name is Malvarius. I overheard his name when trying to take the amulet."

"Malvarius?" Commander Thorne raised an eyebrow, clearly intrigued. "Tell me more."

Mr. Brogath dove into his own well of creativity, weaving an intricate web of falsehoods. "He's tall and thin, with a long, twisted beard," he described, gesturing with his paws to emphasize his words. "His eyes are like two burning coals, and he wears a cloak made of shadows that seems to absorb all light around him."

"Interesting," Thorne said, his brow furrowing as he considered this new information. "But why would he attack our kingdom? What does he want?"

"Power," Mr. Brogath replied without missing a beat. "He seeks control over the entire realm, and this kingdom stands in his way. I've heard whispers of his nefarious schemes during my travels – but I swear, I'm no ally of his! He's the one who cursed me, remember?"

As the words spilled from his mouth, Mr. Brogath marveled at how easily the lies flowed. Was this a hidden talent he'd possessed all along, locked away within the recesses of his forgotten past? The thought both thrilled and alarmed him.

Commander Thorne stared intently at Mr. Brogath, his eyes searching for any hint of deceit. He seemed to be weighing the raccoon's words carefully, considering their merit. Before he could voice his thoughts, however, a frantic messenger burst into the room, panting heavily.

"Commander Thorne!" the messenger gasped. "King Elgron needs you at the front lines immediately! The battle has intensified, and we're losing ground!"

"Understood," Thorne replied, frustration clear in his gravelly voice, his face hardening with resolve. He turned back to Mr. Brogath, his eyes narrowing. "We will continue this discussion later. In the meantime, I suggest you think long and hard about what you've told me – and whether or not it's in your best interest to stick to your story."

With that, Commander Thorne strode from the room, leaving Mr. Brogath alone in the dimly lit cell. As the door slammed shut behind him, the raccoon slumped against the cold stone wall, his heart pounding in his chest.

He had bought himself some time, but at what cost? With each lie he spun, he felt as though he was drifting further away from the truth of who he really was. Would he ever be able to find his way back?

As the distant sounds of battle echoed through the dark corridors, Mr. Brogath couldn't help but wonder if he'd just sealed his own fate.

CHAPTER THREE

The dank stench of the castle dungeons hung heavy in the air, like a noose tightening around Mr. Brogath's neck.

"Unbelievable!" Mr. Brogath muttered under his breath."

His tiny heart pounded relentlessly in his chest. "Think!" he chided himself. "There must be something I can do!"

Just then, an unfamiliar woman passed by, crouched in the shadows of the castle hallway, her eyes scanning the dimly lit corridor for any signs of movement. The cold draft seemed to whisper dark secrets as it brushed against her face, a chilly reminder of the treacherous mission she had undertaken.

"King Elgron's secrets won't remain hidden for long," she vowed silently. With cat-like stealth, she crept forward, her heart pounding with adrenaline.

As she turned to look in the cell, her eyes met Mr. Brogath's.

"By the gods!" she whispered, her eyes widening at the

sight of a raccoon frantically searching for an escape route. "What on earth is this creature doing here?"

"Who's there?" Mr. Brogath demanded, his voice trembling with both fear and hope. He looked up at the unfamiliar figure, his beady black eyes pleading for assistance.

"You can talk? Quieten your voice or you'll get us both caught," she warned in hushed tones. "My name is Seraphine. I may be able to help you, but first I need some answers. Why are you locked up in King Elgron's dungeon?"

"King Elgron thinks I'm the wizard's spy," Mr. Brogath admitted, his whiskers twitching with unease. "I was captured and brought here with the perfect timing to make it look that way."

Lady Seraphine studied him for a moment, her gaze filled with suspicion and curiosity. She couldn't put her finger on it, but something about this raccoon intrigued her. Could he prove useful to their cause?

"Listen carefully," she instructed, her voice low and determined. "I can help you escape, but in return the rebellion needs your help. We're fighting against King Elgron, and we could use someone with... unique abilities."

"Unique abilities?" Mr. Brogath questioned, his brow furrowing in confusion. "I'm not sure what you mean, but if it means freedom from this prison, then you have my word."

"Excellent," Lady Seraphine replied, a hint of a smile playing at her lips. "Now hold tight, for things are about to get interesting."

With that, she withdrew a set of lock picks from her cloak, deftly maneuvering them within the cell's lock. Mere moments later, there was an audible click, and the door creaked open. Mr. Brogath stared in awe, impressed by her skill.

"Quickly, follow me," Lady Seraphine urged, their whispered conversation giving way to silent determination. As they navigated the shadowy halls, Mr. Brogath couldn't help but wonder what he had gotten himself into. The rebels' motives were shrouded in mystery, their goals both enticing and frightening.

"Where are you taking me?" Mr. Brogath asked hesitantly, struggling to keep up with Lady Seraphine's swift pace.

"Somewhere safe," she answered cryptically, her eyes alight with purpose. "But first, we must retrieve the intel I came down here for. Stay close and stay quiet."

As they continued their daring escape, the weight of the decision he had made began to settle upon Mr. Brogath's furry shoulders. He was about to be part of something much larger than himself. And there was no going back.

As they hurried through the dimly lit corridors, Mr. Brogath found himself questioning the wisdom of his decision to follow Lady Seraphine. His heart pounded furiously in his chest, a sensation he found both thrilling and terrifying. The cool stone floor beneath his padded feet provided little comfort as the weight of uncertainty pressed down upon him.

"Wait," he whispered, coming to an abrupt halt. Lady Seraphine glanced over her shoulder, her eyes narrowing in concern. "I appreciate your help, truly, but I'm not sure I'd be useful to your cause. I don't remember anything about my past, and I don't have any unique abilities to speak of."

Lady Seraphine sighed, her breath visible in the cold air. She turned to face him fully, her gaze serious but understanding. "I know this is a lot to ask of you, especially given your memory loss. But we're not just fighting for ourselves; we're fighting for the future of this kingdom. King Elgron's rule has been nothing short of tyrannical. People are suffering, Mr. Brogath. We need every ally we can find. Besides, with your memory loss, you can't be sure you don't have some kind of magic in you. You're a talking raccoon, after all."

Mr. Brogath hesitated, his mind racing with unanswered questions and doubts. He thought of his time spent locked away in that dank cell, the oppressive darkness threatening to swallow him whole. He didn't want to go back there, but joining an uprising seemed like an equally dangerous path.

"Alright," he conceded, his voice barely audible. "I don't know what use I'll be, but I can't ignore the pain and suffering caused by King Elgron."

"Thank you," she whispered, offering a warm smile that chased away the chill lingering in the air. "Together, we can make a difference. I promise."

As they crept through the castle's winding corridors, Mr. Brogath couldn't help but notice how little he actually knew about the rebellion and its aims. Their motives seemed shrouded in mystery, yet Lady Seraphine seemed so convinced of their righteousness.

"Tell me more about this rebellion," he whispered, his curiosity piqued. "What exactly do you hope to achieve if you unseat King Elgron?"

Lady Seraphine hesitated, her gaze flitting between the shadows cast by flickering torches. "Our goals are... complex. We seek to restore balance to the kingdom, to give power back to the people. There are many ways we hope to achieve this, but for now, secrecy is our greatest weapon."

"Secrecy, huh?" Mr. Brogath mused, his nimble paws twitching with unease. "I don't suppose you can share any of the methods you're using?"

"Ah, well..." Lady Seraphine trailed off, an enigmatic

smile playing on her lips. "Let's just say we have a few tricks up our sleeves. But trust me, Mr. Brogath, you'll learn more as you become one of us."

"Are you sure about this path?" Mr. Brogath whispered, his gaze darting left and right as they approached a fork in the corridor. "It feels like we're walking straight into the lion's den."

"Trust me," Lady Seraphine assured him, her voice a silken whisper that seemed to dance upon the cool night air. "I know these halls like the back of my hand."

She led him down the left passage, and they passed a series of ornately decorated doors, each one hinting at the opulence that lay hidden behind it. Mr. Brogath could sense the secrets lurking within these walls, like whispers carried on the breeze.

"Where are we going?" he asked, his bushy tail flicking side to side with unease.

"To lift some valuable information normally guarded by Elgron's elite personal agents," Lady Seraphine replied, a secretive smile playing on her lips. "With the battle happing outside, with a wizard no less, their secret meeting place is almost surely unguarded."

As they continued through the dimly lit corridors, Mr. Brogath couldn't shake the feeling that he was venturing deeper into the unknown. He still wondered what kind of people would make up this rebellion, and whether he could truly trust them. At the same time, however, there was a thrill that coursed through his veins at the thought of joining a cause that could change the fate of the kingdom. His own enthusiasm caught him by surprise. Perhaps he was learning something about his past self.

"Are there any others in your rebellion... like me?" he ventured, his curiosity piqued.

"There aren't any other talking raccoons, if that's what you mean. Each member is unique," Lady Seraphine answered, her voice full of pride. "We all have our own strengths and talents. And we stand united in our desire to overthrow King Elgron and restore freedom to our land."

"Freedom," Mr. Brogath murmured, the word resonating within him like a powerful spell.

As they approached an unremarkable wooden door at the end of the corridor, Lady Seraphine paused, her hand resting on the handle. She turned to Mr. Brogath, her eyes locked onto his with serious intensity.

"Once we step through this door, you need to be prepared for anything," she warned. "Are you prepared for what lies ahead?"

Mr. Brogath hesitated for only a moment before nodding firmly. Whatever challenges awaited him, he would face them head-on, driven by his newfound purpose and the hope of reclaiming his lost memories.

"Let's do it," he said, his voice laced with determination.

Lady Seraphine nodded and opened the door, revealing a hidden chamber filled with darkness. As they stepped inside, the door closed behind them with a soft click, leaving Mr. Brogath with a sense of anticipation that clung to him like a second skin.

Unfortunately, they were not alone. Several hostile figures moved in the dark, their weapons glinting even in the faint light. It seemed that the room was not empty after all. Some of Elgron's elite agents had remained behind to guard the valuable information Lady Seraphine sought.

"We have to get out of here," Mr. Brogath said urgently, his heart pounding in his chest as he realized the danger they were now in. Seraphine was already one step ahead of him.

Without another word, she grabbed his arm and pulled him into a run, heading back down the hallway they had just traversed. He could hear the sound of pursuit behind them as Elgron's guards followed close at their heels. Mr. Brogath had never been more grateful for his raccoon form as it allowed him to move through the darkness easily, if only because he could see clearly. If only he were faster.

Just as they rounded a corner, one of Elgron's men caught up with them and grabbed hold of Mr. Brogath by his tail with an iron grip. Lady Seraphine whirled around, drawing a long and thin sword with blinding speed! She lunged forward in an instant, slicing across the man's forearm. Unprepared, he lost his grip and clutched at his bleeding arm.

Mr. Brogath was stunned by Lady Seraphine's skill, but before he could fully process what had happened they were running again. The bangs of boots on stone were getting louder and closer, and the hallway seemed to stretch out endlessly ahead of them. Yet Seraphine pushed on, her feet barely making a sound against the stone floor. Despite being able to see clearly, and move quietly, the shorter stride was beginning to take a toll.

Finally, they reached an old wooden door at the end of the hallway and Lady Seraphine wasted no time in pushing it open and ushering Mr. Brogath inside. She closed it quickly behind them, and just in time as a guard rounded the corner only seconds later.

The room looked to be some kind of abandoned storage area filled with dusty and crates cleaning supplies. There were no windows or other exits in sight, leaving Mr. Brogath feeling more trapped than ever before. He cast a desperate glance around the room before his eyes settled back onto Lady Seraphine.

She stood tall in the center of the room, her sword held tightly in her hand as she surveyed their surroundings carefully. After a few moments of tense silence, she finally spoke. "We need to get out of here fast. If we hide out in here too long, they'll give up chasing and block the few exits we have. Catch your breath while you can." Her voice was firm and unwavering. There was no hint of panic or fear in her tone.

Mr. Brogath couldn't help but admire her composure even in these dire circumstances.

"And if they find us in here?" he asked.

She didn't give him an answer. He could tell it was because she didn't have one.

"Let's move," she said.

CHAPTER FOUR

Lady Seraphine and Mr. Brogath hurtled through the narrow alleyway, their breaths coming in ragged gasps as they tried to put some distance between themselves and the sound of pursuing footsteps closing in. The cobblestones beneath their feet were slick with water that had seeped through the cracks of the walls, illuminated by the dim glow of the torches that barely pierced the gloom.

"Curse those blasted black cloaks!" Seraphine muttered under her breath, her eyes darting left and right as she searched for a suitable escape route. "I didn't expect them to be here at all!"

"Neither did I," panted Mr. Brogath sarcastically, his raccoon-like form bounding along beside her, struggling to keep up with her long-legged stride. "But it seems we've stumbled upon something important."

"Indeed." Seraphine briefly met his gaze, her eyes gleaming with mischief. "I suppose you could've taken your chances in the prison cell."

Mr. Brogath's heart pounded in his chest, not just from

the exertion of their flight but also from the excitement of this new experience.

"Fair enough! Is there any way to shake them off our trail?" he asked, casting a worried glance over his shoulder at the fast-approaching footsteps. "These guys can run forever."

"Leave that to me," Seraphine replied, flashing him a confident grin that belied the cold sweat on her brow. She abruptly veered into a corridor to their left, dragging Mr. Brogath along with her, and together they dashed down a series of twisting, turning passageways that seemed to lead further and further into the heart of darkness.

"Are you sure you know where we're going?" Mr. Brogath gasped, his little legs burning with exertion as he tried to match Seraphine's relentless pace.

"Trust me," she replied, her voice strained but steady. "I've lost pursuers in these dark tunnels before." As they turned another corner, she added softly, almost to herself, "I just hope we can do it again."

Mr. Brogath trusted Lady Seraphine implicitly, despite the doubts that nagged at him. After all, what choice did he have? He knew she had her reasons for joining the rebellion, but he couldn't help wondering what those reasons were - and if they justified the risks she was taking. But for now, there was no time to ponder such questions. They had to focus on escaping the merciless black cloaked figures who seemed determined to hunt them down without fail.

With every turn, the labyrinth seemed to close in on them. Seraphine dared a glance behind her, and her heart skipped a beat. The black cloaked figures were still close, their footsteps growing louder with each passing second.

"Seraphine," Mr. Brogath panted, his small raccoon

body struggling to keep up with her longer strides. "I'm not sure how much longer I can keep this up."

"Listen carefully, Mr. Brogath" Seraphine whispered, her eyes flicking back and forth between the raccoon and the distant figures. "I need you to hide in the cell. It's me they're after. I'll come back for you once I've lost them, alright?"

"Leave me?" Mr. Brogath asked. Though his protest was half-hearted. He knew full well this was the best strategy she could come up with in the moment.

"Trust me," she pleaded, her voice cracking with the weight of her decision. "I won't abandon you, but if they catch us together, it's over for both of us."

Mr. Brogath hesitated for a moment, fear and uncertainty swirling in his eyes. But he could see the resolve in Seraphine's expression, and with a heavy heart, he nodded. "Alright, Seraphine. I trust you."

"Thank you," she whispered. She quickly opened the door to the cell and helped Mr. Brogath inside. "Stay hidden and stay quiet. I'll be back for you as soon as I can."

"Be careful, Seraphine," Mr. Brogath said, his voice barely above a whisper.

"I will," she promised before shutting the door and turning to leave once again.

Before Seraphine made it two steps, she suddenly produced a pamphlet from her pocket and threw it into the cell with him. With a nod, Seraphine sprinted away once more, her heart pounding as much from fear as from exertion. It was clear to Mr. Brogath in that moment just how much he'd been slowing her down.

Left alone in the dimly lit cell, Mr. Brogath unfolded the pamphlet with shaking paws. He sat down on the cold stone floor, the chill seeping into his bones as he began to read. The words on the page painted a vivid picture of the kingdom's history and the reasons behind the rebellion – tales of tyranny, suffering, and injustice at the hands of King Elgron. A recruiting pamphlet for the rebellion, and an effective one. His eyes widened in shock as he took in each horrid detail, feeling the weight of truth settle heavily upon him.

"By the gods," he murmured under his breath, his thoughts swirling like a tempest. How could a king have been so blind to the suffering around him? In that instant, his sympathy towards the rebels and their cause grew exponentially. How long would it be before his cruelty reached Lily's village too?

He knew now that when Seraphine returned, he would not nag her with more questions. This pamphlet told him everything he needed to know.

Seraphine's heart pounded in her chest as she sprinted down the narrow corridors, her breaths deep and frequent. The distant echoes of the black cloaked figures' footsteps spurred her on, their sinister presence a constant threat at her back.

"Can't stop now," she muttered, gritting her teeth and pushing herself to run faster. "Must lose them."

She weaved through the twisting corridors of the vast castle dungeon, her nimble feet expertly avoiding debris and puddles of murky water. One misstep could result in a twisted ankle or worse, but she couldn't afford to slow down. Not with the others, and now Mr. Brogath, depending on her.

"Think, Seraphine, think!" she scolded herself as she

rounded a sharp corner, her thoughts racing just as fast as her legs. "You've been in tighter spots than this before. But how did you get out?"

Her mind flashed back to her training with the rebels, and the countless hours spent honing her agility and cunning. She recalled one particular lesson when her mentor had emphasized the importance of knowing one's surroundings and using them to one's advantage.

"Use the environment," she whispered, her eyes darting around the dimly lit passage for any opportunity to throw off her pursuers.

Spotting a stack of wooden crates piled haphazardly against a wall, Seraphine seized her chance. With a swift kick, she sent the crates tumbling into the path behind her, creating an obstacle that would hopefully slow down the black cloaked figures.

"Let's see them get past that!" she said triumphantly, allowing herself a fleeting grin.

Breathing heavily, Seraphine forced herself onward, taking several abrupt turns in an attempt to disorient her pursuers further. As she paused briefly to catch her breath, she strained her ears, listening for any sign of the black cloaked figures.

Nearly silent. The hammer of footsteps grew further away, rather than closer. Had she finally lost them?

Cautiously, Seraphine retraced her steps, peering around each corner with bated breath, her senses on high alert. The dungeon remained eerily quiet, and she allowed herself a small sigh of relief.

"Seems like they're gone... for now," she thought, her shoulders sagging with the weight of her accomplishment. "But I can't let my guard down yet. I still need to retrieve that raccoon."

Seraphine set off once more towards the cell where she had left Mr. Brogath, her mind racing with plans and contingencies. She knew their journey was far from over, but at least they had won this particular battle, however small. She'd meant to show him some of King Elgron's secret rooms, believing them to be unoccupied. With the attack going on outside, why were members of an elite unit gathered into a room in the dungeon? Was this little raccoon that much of a concern to them? Having met him, she was convinced he had no idea they were likely preparing for him. He was fortunate she'd provided this distraction, and opportunity to escape.

"Stay strong, Mr. Brogath," she whispered, her voice tinged with both hope and fear. "We'll be out of here soon, together."

While Seraphine raced through the dungeon, Mr. Brogath sat in his cell, turning the crumpled pamphlet over in his paws. The torchlight flickered against the cold stone walls, casting eerie shadows as he read.

"King Elgron... tyranny... lies," he muttered to himself, his whiskers twitching with every revelation. "But why? What does he gain from this?"

Mr. Brogath glanced around the cell, the reality of his surroundings hitting him like a ton of bricks. He could feel the dampness seeping into his fur, the chill in the air making him shiver.

"Is this what the people have been enduring?" he thought, anger bubbling up inside him. "And yet, how do I know if I can trust these rebels? Who's to say they're any better?"

He shook his head, trying to clear his thoughts. There were too many questions, and not enough answers. But one thing was certain: he couldn't stay locked up in this cell forever.

"Seraphine said she'd be back for me," he reminded himself, willing his heart to steady. "I'll just have to trust that she knows what she's doing."

The sound of footsteps echoed down the corridor, and Mr. Brogath tensed, clutching the pamphlet tightly. His heart raced, uncertain whether it was Seraphine or their pursuers approaching.

"Mr. Brogath, are you alright?" Seraphine's voice called out, her breathlessness betraying her haste.

"Ah, Lady Seraphine!" Mr. Brogath exclaimed, relief washing over him. "You made it back!"

"Of course I did," she replied, her fingers working expertly on the lock. "Now come on, we don't have much time. They probably think I already escaped and gave up for now, but we need to move quickly."

As they slipped out of the cell, Mr. Brogath couldn't help but feel an odd mix of trepidation and excitement. His future was uncertain, but for the first time in his new life, he felt like he had a purpose.

"Alright, Lady Seraphine," he whispered, his raccoon eyes glinting with resolve. "Lead the way."

CHAPTER FIVE

The moon shone dimly through a clouded sky as Mr. Brogath and Lady Seraphine made their way through the castle's dimly lit corridors. With Seraphine's expert guidance, they managed to avoid the patrolling guards, eventually finding themselves outside the castle walls and into the safety of the night. Mr. Brogath, still adjusting to his abrupt new circumstances, couldn't help but feel fortunate.

"Thank you for helping me escape," Mr. Brogath whispered to Seraphine as they moved through the shadows. "I must admit, I never thought I'd be so good at scurrying."

Seraphine smiled but quickly turned serious. "You should know that some of the others may not be welcoming of you at first. No one has ever seen a creature like you before, and people tend to be afraid of what they don't understand."

"Understandable," Mr. Brogath replied, his dark eyes thoughtful. "I suppose I'll have to give them time to warm up to me."

"Indeed," Seraphine agreed. "But trust me, they will see your worth soon enough."

With that, the duo continued their journey through the dense forest, guided only by the faint moonlight. After what felt like hours of trekking, they finally reached the hidden rebel camp.

Nestled deep within the ancient woodland, the camp was a marvel of ingenuity and camouflage. The tents, made of sturdy canvas dyed to match the foliage, blended seamlessly with the surrounding environment. Treehouses built high in the branches served as lookout posts and storage areas, while a small network of tunnels ensured a quick escape if needed.

As they entered the heart of the camp, Mr. Brogath took note of the soft glow of lantern light streaming from the tents, casting eerie shadows on the forest floor. He could hear the murmurs of hushed conversations and the occasional laughter that reminded him of the camaraderie these rebels shared.

"Welcome to our humble abode," Seraphine said with a wry smile as she gestured around the camp. "It may not be much, but it's the best we can do with limited resources."

Mr. Brogath nodded, impressed by their resourcefulness. He couldn't help but feel a mixture of curiosity and apprehension as he took in his surroundings. Soon enough, he would have to face the wary eyes of these rebels, and he could only hope that Seraphine was right – that given time, they would see him as an ally rather than a threat.

"Let's get you settled in," Seraphine suggested. "We'll introduce you to the others in the morning when everyone's had some rest. For now, just try to relax."

"Relax," Mr. Brogath mused aloud, his whiskers twitching. "That's something I haven't done yet today."

"Then you're long overdue," Seraphine replied with a knowing smile, leading him to a small tent near the edge of the camp where he could rest before facing the challenges ahead.

The morning sun filtered through the trees, casting dappled shadows on the forest floor as Mr. Brogath cautiously emerged from his tent. He was greeted by the curious stares of rebels who had never seen a talking raccoon before, and he couldn't help but feel exposed under their scrutiny.

"Hey, everyone!" Seraphine called out, drawing their attention away from Mr. Brogath. "This is our new recruit, Mr. Brogath. He's here to help us in our fight against King Elgron."

"Help us?" one of the rebels scoffed. "An interesting pet choice, but how can a raccoon help us?"

"Ah, I may be small, but I assure you, I am quite resourceful," Mr. Brogath replied, trying to sound confident despite his uncertainty.

"It can talk!" another rebel shouted, nearly falling over a stool behind him.

"Calm down," Seraphine said. "He's clearly magical in some way, but he was locked up in Elgron's dungeon after being interrogated by Commander Thorne himself. Clearly they aren't friends, and an enemy of King Elgron's is likely to make a good friend of ours.

"Show us some of your skills," the first rebel suggested. "If you're really an asset, then prove it."

"Very well," Mr. Brogath conceded, his gaze flicking between the rebels and Seraphine, who gave him an encouraging nod.

He scampered up a nearby tree with ease and balance, garnering a few impressed murmurs from the rebels. Then, he leaped from branch to branch, demonstrating his agility. But when he landed back on the ground, he could tell they still weren't convinced.

"Alright, so you can climb trees," the second rebel said, unimpressed. "Even if you were just a normal pet raccoon you could've done that. But what about fighting? Can you hold your own in battle?"

"Battle?" Mr. Brogath hesitated. The word felt strange on his tongue, yet oddly familiar. He tried to push aside the vague memories that stirred within him. "I... I believe I can," he replied, hoping his determination would be enough.

"Then show us," the first rebel challenged, tossing a wooden sword to Mr. Brogath.

Catching it in his paws, Mr. Brogath stared at the weapon, feeling its unfamiliar weight. He felt himself drawn to stories of war and heroism, yet now, faced with the reality of combat, his heart yearned for peace. But he knew he couldn't back down. These rebels needed his help – and perhaps, in helping them, he could find the answers he sought about his own past.

"Alright," Mr. Brogath said, taking a deep breath. "Let's see what I can do."

As he squared off against one of the rebels, Mr. Brogath felt the eyes of the camp upon him. Their suspicion hung heavy in the air, but he was determined to prove himself. The conflict raging within him mirrored the struggle he now faced: a desire for peace coupled with a strange affinity for war. And as the wooden swords clashed, sending echoes through the forest, Mr. Brogath realized that perhaps this battle was not just about winning the rebels' trust, but also understanding who he truly was – and who he wanted to become.

"Come on, Mr. Brogath! You can do this!" Seraphine encouraged from the sidelines.

"Thank you, Lady Seraphine," he replied, trying to keep his focus on the opponent before him. The rebel moved quickly, but Mr. Brogath found his raccoon reflexes were up to the task – albeit in a somewhat clumsy manner. At least he didn't go down with the first strike.

"Watch your footwork!" a stern voice called out. A tall, muscular man with a braided beard approached, scrutinizing Mr. Brogath's movements. He introduced himself as Gareth, one of the rebels' instructors. "You have potential, but your technique needs work."

"Any advice would be appreciated," Mr. Brogath responded gratefully.

"First, try keeping your balance by spreading your legs wider," Gareth instructed. With each tip, Mr. Brogath felt his confidence growing, even as the initial awkwardness remained.

As the days went on, Seraphine and the other rebels began to warm up to Mr. Brogath. They shared their stories around the campfire, offering insight into their cause and their dreams of a better world. One night, an older woman named Elara spoke of her village, which had been destroyed by forces loyal to King Elgron.

"Many of us here have lost everything," she said, gazing into the flames. "But we still believe in a brighter future – one free of tyranny and oppression."

"Elara is right," Seraphine chimed in, placing a comforting hand on the older woman's shoulder. "We fight not just for ourselves, but to honor the memories of those who are no longer with us. We must be their voice."

Listening to their words, Mr. Brogath began to understand the true depth of the rebels' cause. He realized that their struggle was not simply about winning battles, but about standing up for what was right – even in the face of seemingly insurmountable odds.

"Thank you for sharing your stories with me," Mr. Brogath said softly. "I may not remember who I am or where I come from, but I can stand with you now and help build a better world."

"Welcome to our cause, Mr. Brogath," Seraphine smiled warmly. "Together, we will make a difference."

As Mr. Brogath continued to train and learn from the rebels, he felt his connection to their cause – and to himself – growing stronger each day. Though he still longed for peace, he knew that sometimes, one must fight in order to protect what truly matters. And with each swing of his wooden sword, Mr. Brogath moved closer to understanding not only the world around him but also the heart of the raccoon who needed to become a warrior.

"Mr. Brogath, I think it's time you were properly outfitted," Seraphine announced one morning after a particularly intense training session. "Come with me."

She led Mr. Brogath to a small storage shed, its walls lined with various weapons and armor. In the dim light, she selected a simple, crude sword - but reliable and effective all the same.

"Here," she said, handing him the weapon. "This sword

has been passed down through many of our ranks. It's nothing fancy, but it has served us well."

"Thank you, Lady Seraphine," Mr. Brogath replied, grasping the hilt of the sword, a part of him hoping he'd wielded one before losing his memories and that this one would help bring them back. To his disappointment, the weapon felt foreign and uncomfortable in his hand, despite his earlier feelings of being at ease around war. He frowned, confusion clouding his features.

"Something wrong?" Seraphine asked, noticing his discomfort.

"I... I don't know," Mr. Brogath admitted. "I expected the sword to feel more... familiar, somehow. But it doesn't."

"Ah, well," Seraphine chuckled gently. "Perhaps it's simply that you've never held a real sword before. Don't worry, you'll get used to it soon enough."

Next, Seraphine helped Mr. Brogath into a set of armor, made from rough leather and offering minimal protection but allowing for flexibility and speed. As he adjusted the straps and buckles, Mr. Brogath couldn't shake the feeling that something was amiss.

"Is everything alright, Mr. Brogath?" Seraphine inquired, concern evident in her voice.

"Truthfully, I'm not sure, Lady Seraphine," he confessed. "I have this strange sensation – a familiarity with war, but an unfamiliarity with its trappings. I can't quite put my... paw on it."

"Perhaps it's simply another part of your mysterious past," Seraphine suggested. "Maybe you were involved in conflict, but in a different role or capacity. The important thing is that you're here with us now, and we'll help you every step of the way."

"Thank you," Mr. Brogath said, his gratitude genuine.

He looked down at the sword and armor, then back up at Seraphine. "I may not know who I was, but I'm determined to become someone worthy of this cause – and of your trust."

"Then let's get started," Seraphine grinned, her eyes twinkling with determination. "With time and training, I have no doubt you'll become an invaluable member of our rebellion. Together, we will bring justice to our land and create a brighter future for all."

The sun dipped low in the sky, casting long shadows over the rebel camp. Mr. Brogath stood in a small clearing, facing an old straw dummy that was patched together from discarded clothing and stuffed with hay. Sweat trickled down his fur as he gripped the hilt of his sword, trying to recall any memories of wielding a weapon like this before.

"Alright, Mr. Brogath," called out a voice from behind him. He turned to see Seraphine standing next to a grizzled man with a scar running across his cheek – one of the rebellion's sword trainers. "I've asked Master Tyrell here to assess your progress with the blade."

"Progress?" Mr. Brogath repeated, raising an eyebrow. "That might be a stretch, Lady Seraphine."

"Let's just see what you can do," she replied with a smile. "Remember, we're all on the same side here."

Mr. Brogath nodded and turned back to the straw dummy, his paws feeling clumsy and unsure on the hilt of the sword. As he took a deep breath and focused his attention, he couldn't help but wonder why something so familiar felt so foreign at the same time.

"Unleash your inner warrior, Mr. Brogath!" Master Tyrell barked, breaking his concentration.

"Right," muttered Mr. Brogath under his breath. With an awkward lunge, he swung the sword at the dummy — only to miss entirely.

"By the gods," Tyrell sighed, shaking his head. "You swing that sword like a blind mole."

"Ah, well," Mr. Brogath said sheepishly, "Beginner's luck?"

"Or lack thereof," Tyrell grumbled. "But don't worry, we'll make a fighter out of you yet."

Over the next few hours, Mr. Brogath trained tirelessly under Tyrell's watchful eye. He struggled to find a rhythm with the sword, constantly fumbling and missing his marks. During breaks in training, he would often sit alone, pondering the strange duality of his familiarity with war and his incompetence with its weapons.

"Are you alright, Mr. Brogath?" Seraphine asked as she approached him during a break. "You seem... troubled."

"Truth be told, I am," he admitted. "I can't understand why something that feels like it should come naturally is so difficult for me. It's as if there's a part of me that under-stands conflict, but not how to fight in it."

"Maybe your past self was more of a strategist than a soldier," Seraphine suggested. "Or perhaps you played a different role in times of war."

"Perhaps," Mr. Brogath conceded. "But it doesn't change the fact that I'm struggling here and now."

"Give it time," Seraphine reassured him. "We all have our strengths and weaknesses. Maybe you just haven't found yours yet."

"Thank you, Lady Seraphine," Mr. Brogath said, his

voice full of gratitude. "Your kindness and support mean more to me than you know."

Mr. Brogath continued to train with Master Tyrell, making slow but steady progress. His once-clumsy swings became more fluid, and his footwork improved. With each small victory, he felt a growing sense of belonging among the rebels – and a renewed determination to find his place within their ranks.

"Better," Tyrell grunted one day after a particularly successful sparring session. "Still not perfect, but much better."

"High praise from you, Master Tyrell," Mr. Brogath panted, wiping sweat from his brow. "I'll take it."

"Keep at it, Mr. Brogath," Seraphine called out from the sidelines, her eyes full of pride and encouragement. "You're a quick study, just as I suspected."

"Thank you, Lady Seraphine," he replied, his heart swelling with determination. "I won't let you down."

The next day, as Mr. Brogath practiced his swordplay against a wooden dummy, he noticed that he was moving with more grace and precision than before. The once-alien weight of the weapon now felt like an extension of his own arm.

"Look at you go!" Seraphine said, her voice brimming with enthusiasm. "You're really getting the hang of it."

"Indeed," Mr. Brogath replied, panting. "It's starting to feel... easier, somehow."

"Easier" wasn't quite the right word for it. In truth, wielding the sword stirred something deep within him – something he couldn't quite put his finger on, even though he was still certain he wasn't a warrior in his past. But whatever it was, it propelled him forward, driving him to push himself harder and reach new heights in his training.

"Watch me," Tyrell instructed as Mr. Brogath struggled to master a particularly complex combination of moves. The swordmaster demonstrated the sequence with ease, his movements fluid and graceful. "Like this. You're thinking too much. Let your instincts guide you."

"Instincts, right," Mr. Brogath mused, trying to relax his mind and focus on the rhythm of the movements. As he repeated the sequence, he found himself slipping into a kind of trance, his body flowing effortlessly from one motion to the next.

"Excellent!" Tyrell exclaimed, clapping him on the back. "That's it, Mr. Brogath! That's what I've been trying to teach you all along."

"Mr. Brogath," Seraphine said as they sat by the fire, "I'm proud of how quickly you're adapting. But our fight against King Elgron is about far more than fighting. We need to prepare for the challenges ahead – and that means knowing our enemy."

"Indeed," Mr. Brogath agreed, his eyes reflecting the dancing flames. "But I don't even know myself. The fact that I haven't met a single person who knows me makes this even more of a puzzle. You'd think someone would've at least heard of something as strange as a talking raccoon."

"Then let's solve that puzzle together," Seraphine said, her voice resolute. "We'll uncover the truth. About who you are and where you came from."

"Thank you, Lady Seraphine," Mr. Brogath said softly, touched by her unwavering support.

"Unfortunately, after tonight, I won't be back at the camp for a while. I do my best work in espionage, and I can't be gone so long as to compromise my position as a servant in the castle."

"I understand," Mr. Brogath said. "After all, if you weren't there, I wouldn't be here. Who knows what would've happened to me in that dungeon. I hope you're able to find the information you were looking for."

"We'll meet again soon, Mr. Brogath," she said, smiling and placing a hand on his shoulder.

"It's a promise," Mr. Brogath said.

CHAPTER SIX

The rebel camp was a cacophony of tinny laughter and clanging swords, nestled within the embrace of towering oak trees. Tents of various shapes and sizes were scattered haphazardly across the clearing, their patchwork canvas flapping merrily in the breeze. A smoky haze hung low in the air as the smell of roasting meat and bubbling stew wafted from the makeshift kitchen. It was here that Mr. Brogath had found himself for the past few weeks, feeling more at home with each passing day.

"Watch your footing, Mr. Brogath!" called out a gruff voice from the side. "You're not going to land any hits if you keep tripping over your own paws!"

"Right, right," Mr. Brogath muttered under his breath, his whiskers twitching with determination. He lunged forward once more, this time landing a solid hit on his opponent's wooden shield. A grin spread across his face, revealing sharp teeth. "How was that?"

"Better!" The gruff voice belonged to a burly man with a bushy beard and a scar running down his cheek. "But don't get too cocky. You've still got a long way to go."

"Thanks for the encouragement, Dorn," said Mr. Brogath, rolling his eyes. Though he knew Dorn meant well, he couldn't help but feel a little irked by the constant reminders of his inexperience... however correct they were. Despite this, Mr. Brogath was committed to honing his skills and helping the rebellion overthrow the tyrannical King Elgron.

As he continued practicing, Mr. Brogath couldn't help but overhear snippets of conversation from the other rebels. They spoke of their families, their hopes for a better future, and their shared disdain for the so-called "evil" wizard who had been causing trouble throughout the kingdom. Several of the men even boasted they knew of his location beyond the thick forest at the edge of the kingdom. Though he hadn't met the man himself, Mr. Brogath couldn't shake the nagging feeling that there was more to the story than met the eye. No one seemed to have any idea as to the wizard's true motives.

"Alright, break time!" Dorn announced, clapping Mr. Brogath on the back. The raccoon stumbled forward, panting heavily. He accepted a waterskin from one of the other rebels and took a long, grateful swig.

"Thanks," he said, wiping his mouth with the back of a paw. "I needed that."

"Keep up the good work, Mr. Brogath," Dorn replied, giving him an encouraging nod before wandering off to speak with some of the other fighters.

As he rested against a tree trunk, Mr. Brogath couldn't help but feel conflicted about his role in the rebellion.

"Can I really make a difference?" he wondered aloud, staring up at the dappled sunlight filtering through the leaves above. "Or am I just going to end up making things worse?"

A graceful figure approached him, her steps light and confident.

"Hey there!" she called out, her voice bright and energetic. "Mind if I join you?"

Mr. Brogath raised his gaze and studied the newcomer. She was a young woman, perhaps in her early twenties, with short-cropped black hair and large, expressive brown eyes. Her lean frame was clad in simple but well-fitted leather armor, and a thin, curved sword hung at her hip. Anyone could tell she was no stranger to combat.

"Of course not," he replied, straightening up and resting his practice sword on his shoulder. "I'm Mr. Brogath, by the way."

"Rila," she answered, extending a hand for him to shake. "I've heard about you and watched you a bit - the raccoon who can talk and swing a sword. Sounds like quite the story."

"More like a series of increasingly strange events," Mr. Brogath said with a wry chuckle. "But I'm doing my best."

"Good to hear. Tyrell's a fantastic teacher. He even taught Seraphine. Now that he's busy in another part of camp, I'm here to keep you going!"

Over the next several days, Rila and Mr. Brogath trained together, their swords clashing in a shared determination. Rila proved to be an exceptional teacher, guiding Mr. Brogath through new techniques and strategies with patience and enthusiasm. Her self-taught swordsmanship was extremely unorthodox, but surprisingly effective for one without brute force to swing a heavy blade.

"Remember, it's all about balance and timing," she explained as they practiced a particularly challenging maneuver. "You can't just rely on strength or speed alone."

"Easy for you to say," Mr. Brogath grumbled good-naturedly, wiping sweat from his brow. "I'm still getting the hang of this whole 'fighting on two legs' thing."

"Trust me, you're doing great," Rila assured him, flashing a warm smile. "And remember, I have to keep up with the men here, and most of them are a lot bigger and stronger than I am. I'm usually at a strength and speed disadvantage too. You have to work even harder to make up for your disadvantages."

As they trained and exchanged stories, Mr. Brogath found himself growing more and more fond of Rila. She was kind, genuine, and fiercely dedicated. Like many of the rebels, she had lost family members to King Elgron's tyranny - but unlike some, she refused to let hatred and bitterness consume her.

"Vengeance won't bring them back," she confided as they sat around the campfire, staring into the flickering flames. "But if we can end this war and create a better future for others, then their sacrifices won't have been in vain."

"Your strength is inspiring, Rila," Mr. Brogath said softly, his heart swelling with admiration. "And I promise I'll do everything in my power to help you achieve that goal."

Just as it was with Lily, Mr. Brogath felt as though he'd found a true friend in Rila. Forged by shared laughter and the unspoken understanding that they were fighting not just for themselves, but for all those who had suffered under King Elgron's rule. Together, they faced each new challenge with determination and resilience, their spirits buoyed by the knowledge that they stood side by side in the struggle for liberation.

"Thank you, Rila," Mr. Brogath murmured. "For everything."

"Hey, don't get all sentimental on me now," Rila teased,

nudging him playfully with her elbow. "We've still got a long road ahead of us. But you know what? I wouldn't want to walk it with anyone else."

"Neither would I," Mr. Brogath agreed, his eyes shining with gratitude and determination. "Neither would I."

The next day, Mr. Brogath and Rila made their way to a meeting, weaving through the bustling camp. The air hummed with energy, a cacophony of laughter and shouted orders mingling with the clang of weapons being sharpened and the rhythmic beat of boots on packed earth.

"Who exactly are we meeting?" Mr. Brogath asked, his curiosity piqued.

"Ah, I haven't told you yet, have I? We're meeting Galen," Rila replied with a grin. "He's the leader of our rebellion."

Apparently Galen hadn't shared Seraphine's interest in him. She made him out to be an important secret weapon, but Galen hadn't even requested a meeting with him since he'd arrived more than a week ago.

As they approached a large tent, Mr. Brogath caught sight of a tall, broad-shouldered figure emerging from within. Galen was an imposing man, with dark hair streaked with silver and sharp, hawk-like features. His eyes were like chips of ice, and Mr. Brogath felt a shiver run down his spine as they locked onto his own.

"Rila, you've brought our newest recruit, I see," Galen said coldly, extending a hand to Mr. Brogath. "I've heard much about your progress. It's an honor to finally meet you. I saw you from afar, training with the others. A talking raccoon is truly a sight to behold."

"Thank you, Galen," Mr. Brogath replied, shaking the proffered hand. "I'm grateful for the opportunity to be a part of this, and for your group saving me from rotting away in that dungeon... or worse."

Galen smiled and nodded. "You're very welcome, but let's not waste time on pleasantries," he said briskly, turning back towards the tent. "There's much to discuss with everyone."

As they entered the dimly lit interior, Mr. Brogath couldn't help but feel a sense of unease. Galen's presence was commanding, but there was something unsettling about him that he couldn't quite put his finger on.

"King Elgron's tyranny must be stopped, that much is clear," Galen began, pacing the tent like a caged lion. "However, there are those who benefit from his rule and would see our rebellion crushed."

"Surely they're in the minority?" Mr. Brogath asked, his brow furrowed.

"Perhaps," Galen admitted, "but even a small group of sympathizers can cause great damage. We must eliminate them before they have a chance to strike. Or worse, relay valuable information to the king"

Mr. Brogath glanced at Rila, who looked troubled but said nothing.

"Eliminate?" he questioned, suddenly uneasy. "You mean..."

"Kill them," Galen stated bluntly, his icy eyes meeting Mr. Brogath's own. "It's the only way to ensure we don't have regrets later. We cannot afford to be merciful."

"Oh? Is it really the only way? I can't help but question that," Mr. Brogath protested, anger flaring within him.

"Make no mistake," Galen replied, "they are enemies of our cause. And we will do whatever it takes to bring about a better future for this kingdom. It's their choice to stand against us."

With that, he turned on his heel and strode out of the tent, leaving Mr. Brogath and Rila silent and aghast.

"Rila..." Mr. Brogath began, struggling to find the words as his mind raced with conflicting emotions. "How can we justify this? Are we any better than King Elgron if we murder innocent people for the crime of simply disagreeing with us, to remove the possibility of them attacking us first or ratting us out to the king?"

Rila looked at him, her eyes filled with sorrow. "I don't know. Galen's never ordered anything like this before. He's been cold at times but... I'm sorry. I need time to think."

The moon was bright in the sky, casting long shadows across the rebel camp as Mr. Brogath tried to make sense of what he'd just heard. As he paced back and forth, he couldn't help but watch Galen speaking with a few of his closest advisors nearby in the open as the meeting, heated at times, continued.

"Those civilians, while they may not wield swords or magic, could still pose a threat if they provide information or support to King Elgron's forces," Galen argued, his voice tense. "A preemptive strike will save us from unnecessary casualties later on."

"This is no way to gain sympathy for our cause, Galen! How will we be any different from King Elgron himself?" one man asked.

"Galen hasn't led us astray yet. This is war, and war sometimes means making difficult decisions. What if we leave them be, only for them to ambush us later, or join King Elgron on the field? We also benefit from filling our stores with supplies. Others will simply believe they were attacked by bandits," another man added.

Mr. Brogath winced at the ruthless logic, his heart heavy with doubt. He had joined the rebellion to fight against tyranny, not to become an alternative instrument of it. Yet he also understood that war was seldom as black-and-white as one would hope. Was Galen's decision truly evil, or merely a terrible necessity?

"Is there no other way?" Mr. Brogath murmured, more to himself than anyone else. Still, Rila seemed to hear him, her eyes flicking toward him with concern before she turned back to listen to Galen's words.

"Sometimes, sacrifices must be made for the greater good," Galen continued, his gaze distant as if envisioning the grim task ahead. "It is never an easy choice, but it is our duty to make it."

"Greater good..." Mr. Brogath muttered. His mind was suddenly filled with vague stories of wars and conflicts, each side claiming to fight for the greater good, only to become indistinguishable from their enemies in the end. Were these books he'd read, perhaps? "Rila," he said, his voice tight with emotion. "Are you hearing this?"

She hesitated, her brows furrowing as she weighed her thoughts. "I won't pretend that I don't have doubts, Mr. Brogath. Especially after what Galen just ordered."

"Then what do we do?" he asked, his raccoon eyes searching hers for answers. "Do we continue to follow a leader who is willing to murder innocents in cold blood out of paranoia?"

"Mr. Brogath," she began, her hand reaching out to touch his shoulder, "I think—"

"Enough!" Galen barked from across the way, having overheard their conversation just as easily as they heard his. His eyes blazed with anger as he stormed over to them. "We do not have time for this kind of doubt and hesitation. If you cannot stomach the harsh realities of war, then perhaps you have no place among us after all. We aren't holding you prisoner here. You're free to go."

"War shouldn't be an excuse to abandon your principles, Galen," Mr. Brogath shot back, his voice firm. "If we lose sight of what we're fighting for, then what's the point?"

Galen stared hard at him, his jaw clenched before he finally spoke. "You are either with us, or against us, Mr. Brogath. I won't pretend I haven't been worried about your presence from the start. I agreed to let you join us because Seraphine vouched for you. Make your choice. Leave, or stay. If you stay, you should stay with the intention of following orders."

As the rebel leader walked away, Mr. Brogath felt torn between loyalty to the cause and his own sense of right and wrong. He looked at Rila, seeking solace in their shared uncertainty, but she could offer him no guidance. He could see that she was just as torn as he was, even though Galen's ultimatum hadn't been directed at her.

"Perhaps," he whispered, his heart heavy with the weight of his decision, "we must find our own way in this world."

***

As the moon rose higher, Mr. Brogath wondered if he would ever truly understand the nature of the conflict surrounding him, or if the line between hero and villain was forever destined to remain obscured by the darkness of this war.

He strolled to the outskirts of the camp and sat quietly on a log, not realizing Rila had followed him the entire way. He gazed out into the forest, suddenly wondering why he, as a woodland creature, didn't feel drawn to it.

Rila approached him carefully, sensing the turmoil that seemed to radiate from him, just as it no doubt did from her.

"Mr. Brogath," she began tentatively, "may I join you?"

He glanced up at her, his eyes reflecting the fading light, and nodded. As she seated herself beside him, she could feel the tension between them.

"Rila," Mr. Brogath said after a moment, "how important is doing the right thing along the way when compared to succeeding at something that will benefit everyone?"

She furrowed her brow, considering his words. "I've always believed that we were fighting for a better world, one free from King Elgron's tyranny. But now, after what Galen's ordered... I'm not so sure how to answer that."

"Neither am I," he admitted, his voice heavy with regret. "I can't help but think that there must be some other way, a better way to oppose the king without becoming monsters ourselves. But I really was almost born yesterday, in a way, so perhaps I am naive."

"Perhaps or perhaps not," Rila said. "We simply need to remind ourselves of who we are and why we fight. We can't let fear or desperation cloud our judgment. It can't be a fight for vengeance. It must be a fight for liberation. A fight for the good of the living, not one seeking revenge for the dead."

As they sat there, debating the morality of their cause, the weight of their choices bearing down upon them, a flicker of doubt began to take hold in Rila's heart as well. She had always been so certain, so confident in her path, but now...

"Mr. Brogath," she asked quietly, "what do you plan to do?"

He sighed, his gaze fixed on the horizon. "I cannot stay

here, not while there is so much uncertainty within me. I need to find my own answers and understand who I truly am in this world."

"Does that mean you'll leave then? The rebellion, I mean." Rila's voice was barely a whisper, her fear of losing him evident.

"Yes," he responded softly, looking into her eyes. "At least for now. I can't fight for a man who is willing to compromise the soul of his cause for victory. And he's right, too. If I'm going to stay, I should be willing to follow his orders and not create discontent for a cause that isn't truly mine. I don't even know where my home is... or was."

Rila swallowed hard, fighting back the tears that threatened to spill over. "I... I understand," she said, her voice cracking. "I wish I could go with you, but..."

"You have your own path to follow, Rila," Mr. Brogath assured her, placing a comforting paw on her shoulder. "You should stay and help guide the rebellion towards a better future."

"Promise me one thing," she implored, her eyes shining with unshed tears. "Promise me that we'll meet again someday."

He hesitated, uncertainty clouding his features, before finally nodding. "I promise. No matter what happens, Rila, we'll meet again."

Mr. Brogath awoke before dawn, the air around him heavy with anticipation and apprehension. He had made his decision, and it was time to put it into action. As he packed his belongings, he couldn't help but think of Lily, the young girl who had found him when he was lost and alone. He wondered what would become of her in this conflict between good and evil – if such distinctions even existed anymore.

"Rila," Mr. Brogath called out softly, not wanting to disturb the slumbering rebels nearby. She stirred from her makeshift bed, rubbing the sleep from her eyes.

"Are you really leaving now?" she asked, her voice thick with sleep and emotion. "It's still dark."

"I must," he replied, his own emotions threatening to surface. "The sooner I go, the sooner I can find answers. I need to understand this world better, figure out where I stand and what I truly believe in. Only then can I hope to return and make a difference. Besides, raccoons can see really well in the dark."

"I had a feeling you wouldn't wait for dawn. Take this," Rila said, pressing a small pouch into his paw. "I saved some food for your journey. It isn't much, but it should keep you going for a few days."

"Thank you," he murmured, moved by her thoughtfulness. "I'll never forget your kindness, Rila."

"Neither will I," she whispered, tears streaming down her cheeks as she embraced him one last time.

They held each other for a moment, knowing it might be the last time they'd feel the warmth of their friendship. With a final nod, Mr. Brogath turned away and began his solitary trek towards the edge of the camp, his heart heavy with the burden of his choices.

As he walked, he could sense the curious gazes of the other rebels upon him, whispering questions and forming hasty conclusions about his departure. He knew that the atmosphere in the camp would become tense and uncertain, but it was a necessary price to pay for the pursuit of truth.

"Hey," called out one of the rebels, a burly man with an unkempt beard. "Where do you think you're going?"

"None of your concern," Mr. Brogath replied tersely, not in the mood for idle conversation.

"Is it true what they say?" the man persisted, ignoring the cold response. "That you're leaving because you don't agree with Galen's methods? That you think we're just as bad as Elgron's lot?"

"Believe what you will," Mr. Brogath said, quickening his pace. He didn't want to engage in any debates – he needed time alone to process everything that had happened and determine his own convictions. He wasn't even sure how to answer the question even if he'd wanted to.

He finally reached the edge of the camp, pausing for a moment to take in the sight of the rebel encampment that had been his temporary home. It was a place of hope and camaraderie, now overshadowed by doubt. As he turned away, he couldn't help but wonder how many more lives would be affected and changed, like Lily's or Rila's, by this struggle for power and survival. Even if just for their sake, he wanted to do something more.

With each step he took away from the camp, Mr. Brogath felt a mixture of freedom and trepidation. The road ahead was uncertain, but he was resolute in his quest for a better path forward.

CHAPTER SEVEN

"By the gods," Mr. Brogath muttered under his breath, "there must be another way to defeat King Elgron." He paced back and forth, his raccoon tail swishing through the air as he pondered the situation. The battle against the tyrant king had been dragging on for who knows how long, and he could no longer bear the thought of more bloodshed.

"Perhaps a visit to the 'evil' wizard in his tower is in order," he decided, pausing mid-pace. Mr. Brogath knew little of the wizard, except that his powers were rumored to be great and terrible. But if there was anyone who might hold the secret to ending the conflict with King Elgron swiftly and peacefully, surely it was him. Not only that, but it was already clear that he and Elgron were not on good terms.

"Ah, and I think I know where this mysterious tower can be found..." Mr. Brogath mumbled aloud. He recalled fragments of gossip he'd overheard in the camp. Whispers of a tower hidden beyond a dark forest, surrounded by treacherous cliffs and an ever-present veil of mist. It was said that the tower itself was made of obsidian, rising like a jagged shadow against the sky.

Likely some of it was exaggeration.

"Sounds like a place worth visiting!" Mr. Brogath exclaimed, his raccoon eyes gleaming with determination. With a final flick of his tail, he set off to find the elusive wizard's lair.

As he ventured farther from the camp, Mr. Brogath's thoughts turned inward, and he couldn't help but question his own identity. "Am I truly just a raccoon, or something more?" he pondered. "Why do I care so deeply about this conflict between humans? And how did I come to possess the mind and voice similar to one?"

He shook his head, forcing himself to focus on the task at hand. The landscape gradually transformed around him, thick trees giving way to the gnarled and twisted trunks of the dark forest. A chill wind whispered through the branches as he entered, his raccoon senses alert for any sign of danger.

"I'll be," Mr. Brogath exclaimed, looking up at the towering trees that surrounded him. "This forest is denser than a monarch's head." But he pressed on, determined to find the wizard and put an end to the senseless war.

Hours passed as he navigated the treacherous terrain, leaping over fallen logs and scrambling up steep inclines. He was no stranger to the wilderness, but even he found this forest to be a formidable challenge. His fur was soon soaked with sweat, and his limbs trembled with exhaustion.

"Curse this blasted forest!" he growled, pausing for a moment to catch his breath. "If I ever get my paws on that wizard, I'll give him a piece of my mind about his choice of real estate."

Despite his frustration, Mr. Brogath couldn't help but marvel at the beauty of the forest: the vibrant greens of the moss-covered rocks, the delicate patterns of lichen that adorned the tree trunks, and the shafts of sunlight that pierced the gloom to illuminate patches of wildflowers like tiny spotlights.

"Ah well," he sighed, resuming his journey, "at least it's scenic."

As he continued deeper in, he remained vigilant, his keen raccoon ears listening for any sound that might betray the presence of the wizard's stronghold. And though the whispers of the camp had provided a rough description of the tower's location, he knew that only by pressing forward would he discover whether the rumors were true or merely the fanciful tales of bored soldiers.

"Obsidian tower and treacherous cliffs," he mused, forging onward, "I'll find you yet, oh mysterious wizard. And when I do... Well, I suppose we'll just have to see what happens then."

The dense foliage of the forest seemed to stretch on forever, with gnarled roots reaching out like greedy fingers, threatening to trip Mr. Brogath at every turn. The air was thick with humidity, and he found himself panting more and more as he traipsed through the underbrush.

"Could this place be any harder to navigate?" he grumbled, pushing aside a low-hanging branch that had been blocking his path. His fur was matted with dirt and sweat, and he couldn't shake the feeling that the entire forest was conspiring against him.

"Perhaps if I climb one of these trees," he thought, "I might get a better view of where I am." With nimble raccoon agility, he scaled a nearby oak, hoping to catch a glimpse of the fabled obsidian tower through the canopy.

But alas, the treetops only offered him a sea of green leaves, swaying gently in the breeze.

"Of course," he muttered, descending back to the ground with a sigh. "Why make things easy, oh mystical forest?"

He stumbled upon a patch of thorny brambles that seemed almost alive, twisting and writhing as they tried to ensnare him. He narrowly managed to free himself with a well-placed swipe of his blade, but not before sustaining a few scratches.

"Ouch! You win this round, spiteful shrubs," he said, wincing as he inspected his wounds.

Later, Mr. Brogath found himself face-to-face with an irritable porcupine, seemingly guarding a narrow pathway deeper into the forest. The prickly creature bared its teeth and hissed at him, unwilling to let him pass.

"Easy there, friend," Mr. Brogath tried to reason, holding up his paws in a placating gesture. "I mean you no harm. I'm just trying to find the wizard's tower."

The porcupine retorted by bristling its quills dangerously.

"Listen," Mr. Brogath said, adopting a more persuasive tone. "I don't want to fight you. But I can't turn back now. I have to find that wizard and put an end to this war."

The porcupine seemed to grumble after a moment, begrudgingly moving aside.

"Thank you," Mr. Brogath replied with a nod, quickly scurrying past the prickly sentry before it could change its mind. Or perhaps he'd just startled the creature by accident. It seemed more fun to imagine it had a motivation.

As he delved deeper into the forest, Mr. Brogath couldn't help but feel a growing sense of unease. The shadows seemed darker here, the silence more oppressive. It was as if the very air was charged with latent magic, daring him to take another step.

"Come on, old raccoon," he murmured to himself, pushing through the lingering tendrils of fear that threatened to slow his progress. "You've faced worse than a spooky forest.

The shadows of the trees seemed to stretch and reach for him, their twisted limbs like gnarled fingers grasping at the air. The sun peeked through the canopy in fleeting moments, casting a dappled light upon the forest floor. It was in one such moment of clarity that he spotted a rustle in the underbrush.

"Who goes there?" he called out, his voice quivering with a mix of curiosity and trepidation.

A raccoon poked its head out from behind a bush, its eyes sparkling with intelligence as it examined Mr. Brogath. The creature chittered softly, its tiny paws reaching out as if seeking connection.

"Ah," Mr. Brogath muttered to himself, "a fellow raccoon." He studied the creature before him, noting the differences between them. This raccoon was smaller, its fur a little ragged, and its eyes held a wildness that Mr. Brogath couldn't quite place within himself. As they locked gazes, he felt an eerie sense of detachment.

"Am I truly a raccoon?" he pondered aloud, feeling the weight of his forgotten past pressing down upon him more than ever in that moment. "Or is this form merely a mask, hiding something deeper, something more profound?"

The raccoon stared back, tilting its head as if considering the question. For a moment, it seemed as though the small creature might hold the answers Mr. Brogath sought. But then, with a flick of its striped tail, it darted away, disappearing into the shadows of the forest.

"Wait!" Mr. Brogath cried, but the raccoon was gone, leaving him alone with his thoughts and doubts.

Heaving a heavy sigh, Mr. Brogath turned his attention to the task at hand: navigating the treacherous forest. Drawing upon the wilderness skills he had learned from his time with Lily and later, Rila, he began to search for signs of a clearer path that would lead him to the wizard's stronghold. This proved to be no small feat, as the forest seemed determined to thwart his progress at every turn.

"Of course," he grumbled, "nothing worthwhile is ever easy."

He encountered more thorny bushes that snagged at his fur, slick rocks that threatened to send him toppling into hidden ravines, and countless dead ends where the trees closed in like prison bars. Through it all, Mr. Brogath persevered, using his newfound resourcefulness to overcome each obstacle.

"Take that, you overgrown shrubbery!" he exclaimed triumphantly as he scaled a particularly stubborn hedge, his claws digging into the thick branches for purchase.

Mr. Brogath's heart pounded against his ribs as he stumbled out of the forest, his legs wobbling like overcooked noodles. The wizard's tower obscured the setting sun, its dark silhouette cutting through the orange sky like a dagger. Mr. Brogath blinked, pausing to catch his breath and steady himself.

"Focus," he muttered, shaking off the weariness that threatened to overwhelm him. "Almost there."

As he trudged across the rolling hills, the landscape morphed from lush greenery to a rocky expanse. The wind whispered in his ears, blowing tufts of fur into his eyes and tickling his whiskers. He squinted ahead, scanning the horizon for any sign of life when he spotted a figure hunched at the edge of a cliff, their back facing him.

"Oi! You there!" Mr. Brogath called out, curiosity piquing at the sight of the stranger.

The figure turned slowly, revealing a gaunt face framed by unkempt shoulder-length brown hair and a bushy beard that hung down to his chest. His skinny body looked half-starved, and he wore nothing but a tattered loincloth that flapped wildly in the wind.

"Ah, greetings, little muse," the man said, his voice wispy yet warm. "I am known as The Bearded Fool. What brings you to these desolate lands?"

"Muse?" He shook his head, refocusing on the task at hand. "I'm here to seek the counsel of the wizard who lives in that tower." He pointed towards the obsidian structure in the distance.

"Ah, the wizard," The Bearded Fool nodded, scratching his chin thoughtfully. "You are a most peculiar raccoon, pursuing such an unusual quest."

"Trust me," Mr. Brogath replied, his whiskers twitching in irritation. "I'm well aware."

"Very well," The Bearded Fool said, his eyes twinkling with mischief as he danced about in a circle around Mr. Brogath. "The past is a cage, little raccoon, but the key lies within you. Embrace it, and your true purpose shall be revealed."

"Riddles?" Mr. Brogath scoffed, his ears flattening against his head. "I don't have time for this nonsense. I need to get to that tower!"

"Patience, little raccoon," The Bearded Fool replied, unfazed by Mr. Brogath's frustration. "In time, all will become clear. Remember, sometimes the greatest wisdom is hidden in the most unexpected places."

"Right, great. Thanks," Mr. Brogath muttered sarcastically, already turning to resume his journey.

"Good luck, little raccoon!" The Bearded Fool called after him, his laughter carried away by the wind. "Fate has chosen you for a reason! Too bad. I have so much more to say!"

"Fine, I'll hear you out," Mr. Brogath sighed, his impatience barely contained. "What is it you want to tell me?"

"Ah, my dear raccoon," The Bearded Fool replied with a broad grin. "The answer you seek will not be found in the tower yonder. It lies within yourself."

"Ridiculous!" Mr. Brogath snapped, flicking his bushy tail in annoyance. "And what do you know of my journey? I've come this far without your help, and I'll see it through on my own."

"Very well," The Bearded Fool said, raising his hands in mock surrender. "But if you change your mind, you know where to find me." He took a step back and bowed dramatically. "For now, at least."

"Wait," Mr. Brogath's curiosity piqued despite himself, his ears perking up. "You're offering to guide me to the wizard's tower?"

"Indeed," The Bearded Fool replied, his expression suddenly solemn. "I know the most direct way, and I can lead you there safely. But I must warn you: the path will not be easy, and the answers you find may not be the ones you expect."

"Is that another riddle?" Mr. Brogath grumbled, narrowing his eyes.

"Merely a truth, little raccoon," The Bearded Fool said softly, his gaze intense before suddenly breaking into another wild dance, shuffling side to side.

"Fine," Mr. Brogath conceded, swallowing his skepticism. "Lead the way. But no more riddles or nonsense, you hear?"

"Of course," The Bearded Fool agreed, a knowing smile tugging at the corners of his lips as he cackled. "Follow me."

As they moved forward, Mr. Brogath couldn't shake the feeling that he was being led into something much bigger than he had anticipated. The Bearded Fool's cryptic advice nagged at him, making him second-guess his decision to accept the stranger's help. Yet, as the tower loomed closer, he couldn't deny that a part of him was eager to uncover the truth - whatever it may be.

"Tell me, little raccoon," The Bearded Fool mused as they walked, "what do you hope to gain from this journey?"

"Answers," Mr. Brogath replied tersely. "But from the wizard, maybe a way to end this conflict without more bloodshed."

"Ah, yes. A noble goal," The Bearded Fool nodded sagely, stroking his unkempt beard. "But remember: sometimes, the greatest victories are won not through force, but through understanding. Some are the opposite. Some are like bark on trees, until they become the sounds that escape from a dog's mouth," he said, cackling loudly to himself.

"Right. That was a good one," Mr. Brogath snapped, clenching his paws in frustration. "Look, I just need to get to the wizard and figure things out from there. Enough with the cryptic ramblings!"

"Very well, little raccoon," The Bearded Fool said, his eyes twinkling. "I will say no more on the matter... for now."

The sun dipped closer to the horizon, casting long shadows across the rugged terrain as Mr. Brogath trudged along behind The Bearded Fool. Though their journey had been arduous thus far, Mr. Brogath couldn't help but feel a growing sense of exhilaration as they neared their destination. But why?

"Watch your step, little raccoon," The Bearded Fool said, his voice lilting with amusement. "These rocks have a habit of tripping up even the most nimble-footed."

"Raccoons are known for their agility," Mr. Brogath replied, his whiskers twitching in annoyance. "I'll manage just fine."

"Ah, yes," The Bearded Fool mused, "but you are not just any raccoon, now, are you?"

Mr. Brogath clenched his jaw, resisting the urge to snap at the enigmatic man once more. Instead, he focused on navigating through the rocky outcroppings and treacherous crevices that littered the landscape. The wizard's tower loomed ever nearer, a dark sentinel against the fading light.

"Almost there, little muse," The Bearded Fool said, his voice barely audible over the howling wind that had begun to whip around them. "Just a short climb up this cliff, and we shall be at the wizard's doorstep."

"Cliff?" Mr. Brogath squeaked, staring up at the imposing vertical wall of rock. "You couldn't have mentioned that earlier?"

"Where would be the fun in that?" The Bearded Fool laughed, beginning to scale the sheer rock face with surprising ease.

Just who was the wild animal here?

"Fun..." Mr. Brogath muttered under his breath, gritting his teeth as he followed suit. His claws dug into the stone, finding purchase where his companion's fingers had left small indentations. Slowly but surely, he made his way upward, each move more precarious than the last.

"Almost there," The Bearded Fool called down to him,

his voice echoing through the wind. "Just a few more steps... grabs? Jumps?"

With a final burst of effort, Mr. Brogath crested the top of the cliff, collapsing onto the flat expanse of rock with a weary huff. Catching his breath, he looked up to see the wizard's stronghold in all its imposing glory: a tall, foreboding tower crafted from black stone, with narrow windows that glowed an eerie green in the twilight. A shiver ran down Mr. Brogath's spine as he took in the sight.

"Welcome to the lair of the reclusive wizard," The Bearded Fool said, a hint of mockery in his tone.

"Thank you," Mr. Brogath replied, still catching his breath. "I couldn't have done it without you."

"Indeed," The Bearded Fool agreed, his eyes gleaming with some unspoken emotion. "And now, little raccoon, it is time for me to take my leave. You must face your destiny alone. Don't worry though, I'll be watching, just as I have been all along." He cackled maniacally as he scratched his beard, flicking his tongue and howling like a madman.

"Wait!" Mr. Brogath cried out, but when he turned his head, The Bearded Fool was gone, vanished as if he'd never been there at all.

Baffled and uneasy, Mr. Brogath steeled himself for what lay ahead. He had come this far seeking answers and a chance for peace; now, it was time to discover whether the enigmatic wizard held the key to both... or either. With determination in his heart, he padded towards the great wooden doors of the tower, ready to face whatever awaited him within.

CHAPTER EIGHT

Mr. Brogath, his small body aching from the rigors of his travel, finally stood before the ominous wooden doors of the wizard's tower. He hesitated, his heart pounding as he gazed at the inscrutable barrier between him and the enigmatic figure within the dark stone structure. Fear gnawed at the edges of his thoughts, yet curiosity burned brighter, driving him to find out if the wizard inside was truly the evil being he had been led to believe.

"Either I'm incredibly brave or incredibly stupid," Mr. Brogath muttered under his breath before giving the door a few hesitant knocks. The sound echoed through the tower, making him wince. "Or both."

To his surprise, the door creaked open, revealing a dimly lit chamber filled with odd trinkets and dusty books. A hunched figure emerged from the shadows, his eyes narrowing as they fell upon the small raccoon visitor.

"Who dares disturb Roth the great wizard?" the wizard boomed, his voice a fierce growl that sent shivers down Mr. Brogath's spine.

"Um, hello there," Mr. Brogath said, trying to muster all the charm he could. "I'm Mr. Brogath, and I've come a long way to meet you. I wanted to see for myself if you were really some evil monster, as so many say."

The wizard threw back his head and laughed, a bitter sound that seemed to shake the very walls of the tower. "Evil? Of course, they say that. King Elgron's propaganda is nothing if not effective." Roth's voice softened, tinged with sadness. "No, little raccoon, I do not think those who know me consider me to be evil. But it seems the world has no place for those who defy its cruel whims... or its cruel tyrants."

As Roth led Mr. Brogath further into the tower, the raccoon couldn't help but notice the cramped living conditions, two old wizards leaned over a table playing some kind of board game, their eyes reflecting a mixture of fear and distrust. He began to realize that Roth was not an evil figure at all, but a protector of these exiled magic users who had been shunned by the world.

"Your living conditions are...not ideal," Mr. Brogath observed, his voice laced with sympathy. "Why do you stay here?"

"Where else would we go?" Roth replied, bitterness creeping into his tone again. "Wastelands, rocks, and water surround the island. We exist on the furthest reaches of what is habitable. These wizards have been used and discarded like broken tools, forced to flee their homes, and feared for their very existence. We hide away from civilization because they would rather see us dead than acknowledge our humanity... and a part of me cannot blame them for it."

"But you still keep tabs on the outside world?" Mr.

Brogath asked, trying to understand the complexity of their situation.

"Only through my crows," Roth answered, nodding towards the birds perched near a window. "They are my eyes and ears in Elgron's kingdom, watching, waiting, and reporting back to me."

Mr. Brogath looked around at the haggard faces of the wizards, each one telling its own story of pain and loss. His heart ached for them, and he knew he had to help in any way he could.

"Roth, I came here believing you may very well be a monster," Mr. Brogath said, shaking his head. "But now I see that you're just trying to protect those who have no one else to turn to. The real monster is out there."

"Tell me more about this kingdom's relationship with magic users," Mr. Brogath asked Roth, his eyes narrowing in concern. "Why is King Elgron so fixated on them?"

"Elgron fears what he cannot control," Roth replied, his voice heavy with emotion. "Magic users are a threat to him and his iron grip on power. He has systematically hunted down and killed any who refused to serve him in oppressing the people of his kingdom. Wizards have a history of being used as weapons of war. We have long lives, and memories just as long. In time, all of us made a secret pact to no longer seek love and produce heirs to follow after us. Magic shall die with the five of us that remain. Barely a month ago, we were six..."

"Such cruelty," Mr. Brogath murmured, his heart aching for the victims of such senseless violence. He felt a wave of sympathy for Roth and his cause; the wizard was merely trying to protect the last remnants of a persecuted group.

"Indeed," Roth agreed, his eyes flickering with anger.

"But I have tried to stop him in my own way. When I learned that Elgron planned to stage a false attack, pinning a terrible crime upon a wizard to further justify his actions, I had to act."

"False attack?" Mr. Brogath questioned, his curiosity piqued.

"Another of his propaganda operations, designed to deceive the public into believing that we, the magic users, were responsible for a heinous act," Roth explained. "It would only serve to deepen the hatred and mistrust against us."

"And you stopped it?"

"Partially... for now," Roth sighed, his face etched with regret. "I risked appearing in person and attacking preemptively with my magic, attempting to save a captured wizard who was to be used as a pawn in the king's scheme. But I was too late. Elgron had her killed before I could reach her. If he could not have her for his own uses, he would not allow her to escape with her life. I only regret that I was driven away by his forces before I could deliver him the same fate."

Mr. Brogath's mind raced with thoughts, each new revelation pushing him further away from his initial assumptions about the wizard before him. It was clear now that Roth was not the villain he had expected, but rather a desperate man trying to protect the last vestiges of his kind from a ruthless ruler.

"Roth," Mr. Brogath said, determination steeling his voice. "Thank you for sharing this with me. I can only imagine the burden you've been carrying all these years."

"Burden or not, I've made it my duty to protect them," Roth replied, his eyes glistening with emotion that threatened to bring him to tears. "They at least deserve to live out their last days in peaceful solitude."

"Then let us fight King Elgron together," Mr. Brogath declared, his voice filled with conviction. "No one should have to suffer as you and your people have. Nor do his citizens deserve to suffer as they do under his tyranny."

Roth only eyed Mr. Brogath with skepticism, though his appreciation was apparent in his faint smile. He could not blame Roth for being skeptical.

Roth's eyes grew distant as he stared out the window, a crow perched on the ledge outside. "Had I not stopped that false attack, it would have turned public opinion against magic users even more. The king's lies would have ignited violence and distrust against us like never before. They might've even come after us themselves."

Mr. Brogath's brow furrowed as he considered the implications. Propaganda was a powerful weapon, and King Elgron seemed to wield it effectively, and without mercy. As if sensing his thoughts, Roth turned back to him.

"Through my crows, I've spied on the king's actions. He had also ordered your execution, Mr. Brogath," Roth revealed, his voice heavy with concern. "But the rebel woman, Seraphine, saved you before it could be carried out. You are truly a creature possessing good fortune. At least on that particular day."

A shiver ran down Mr. Brogath's spine at the thought of his near demise. He owed Seraphine his life, though it seemed she had kept this information from him - perhaps to protect him from further fear or worry, or because she hadn't known it herself. His heart swelled with gratitude and determination, knowing that the rebels needed every ally they could find in their fight against King Elgron's tyranny. Seraphine herself had believed he would help them somehow, after all.

"Seraphine?" Mr. Brogath asked, his voice barely above a whisper. "Is she... safe?"

Roth's expression darkened, and he looked away, his fingers fidgeting with the hem of his robe.

"She was caught and executed upon her return to the castle," Roth said, his voice filled with sadness and anger. "I'm... sorry you had to find out this way."

Mr. Brogath felt a pang of sorrow in his chest. Seraphine had risked everything to save him, and now she was gone. He couldn't help but wonder if he could have done something to prevent her death. His heart was heavy with sorrow and grief as he thought of Seraphine, and how hard she fought to save him, a stranger. Tears welled up in his eyes as he embraced the sorrow overflowing within him.

Then an anger swelled inside him, hot enough to dry his tears, bringing him back into the moment. Recruiting Roth and the other wizards is how he would honor her. She believed in him, after all. That he would make a difference somehow. That he could offer something to her people. Perhaps, in this way, he could.

"We must succeed quickly," Mr. Brogath said, his voice full of determination. "For Seraphine and for all those who have suffered under Elgron's rule. We cannot let her sacrifice be in vain. It's not just the wizards King Elgron threatens, but everyone. We can't be divided any longer."

"I will do everything in my power to aid you in your fight against Elgron," Roth said. "But we must also be smart and strategic. We cannot simply attack head-on and expect to win. We must gather information, plan our moves carefully, and strike when the moment is right."

"Roth," Mr. Brogath began, his voice steady and resolute. "Forgive me for being blunt, but there has been enough planning and caution already. We are past that. We need to act, and quickly. I may not remember my past, but I care about this kingdom's future. I want to help bring peace to this kingdom and put an end to King Elgron's rule. Will you help me do that?"

Roth looked at him, his eyes searching Mr. Brogath's face for any sign of insincerity. But all he found was the unwavering determination that shone in the little raccoon's eyes.

"Your heart seems sincere, Mr. Brogath," Roth replied slowly, weighing his words carefully. "I will do what I can to help, though reluctantly. But know this - it won't be easy. Elgron's army is many times larger than the rebellion, with better training and equipment. Even with the wizards added in, this will not be easy."

"Nothing worth fighting for ever is," Mr. Brogath said, a small smile playing on his lips.

"Truer words are rarely spoken. Go on, then. Lay out this plan of yours," Roth said.

"Roth," Mr. Brogath began, feeling the weight of his words as he laid out his proposal. "I believe we have a common goal - to bring peace to this kingdom and end the senseless hunting of magic users. I've come across a group of rebels who share that same goal. They're fighting against King Elgron's tyranny, and I think we should join forces."

He paused, watching Roth's face for any sign of agreement or dissent. The wizard, however, remained silent, his expression unreadable.

"By allying ourselves with them," Mr. Brogath continued, hoping to sway Roth with the prospect of unity, "we can pool our resources, knowledge, and abilities. Together, we stand a much better chance of toppling King Elgron and creating a lasting peace."

Roth frowned, his brow furrowing in thought as he mulled over Mr. Brogath's suggestion. "It's true that we share the same goals," he conceded slowly, "but I must admit, I have my reservations about joining forces with outsiders who likely distrust us just as much as Elgron himself and will seek to use us for military power just as he has."

"Understandable," Mr. Brogath nodded, acknowledging Roth's mistrust. He took a deep breath, preparing to make his case. "But consider this: if we remain separate, King Elgron will continue to paint magic users as monsters, fueling the people's fear and hatred. By working together with the rebels, we can show the kingdom that magic users are champions of the people, rather than the evil creatures they've been made out to be."

As Mr. Brogath spoke, he could practically see the thoughts running through Roth's mind, the wizard weighing the risks and benefits of such an alliance. It was clear that Roth wasn't entirely convinced, but Mr. Brogath could also see a glimmer of hope in the older man's eyes.

"Think about it, Roth," Mr. Brogath urged. "Together, we can make a real difference in this world, rather than being content with these never-ending cycles of losses and victories that never amount to anything."

The silence that followed was heavy with anticipation as Roth stared at Mr. Brogath, his eyes searching for any hint of deception or hidden motives. What he found, however, was only the earnest determination of a creature who genuinely believed in their cause.

"Alright," Roth said finally, his voice tinged with caution and skepticism. "I will consider your proposal, Mr. Brogath.

But I must discuss it with the other two wizards here before making a decision."

"Of course," Mr. Brogath replied, sitting on a stool and flipping through an old herbalism book. "I am in no hurry to brave that forest again, so take all the time you need."

A gust of wind curled around the wizard's tower, rustling the leaves of nearby trees and causing the aged stones to creak ever so slightly. Mr. Brogath stood beside Roth, watching as the sun dipped below the horizon, casting long shadows across the landscape.

"Very well," Roth said hesitantly, his voice heavy with caution. "You may try to form this alliance with the rebels, but I must insist that we proceed with the utmost care. There are risks involved for all of us. Even beyond Elgron."

"Understood," Mr. Brogath replied, nodding solemnly. He knew that if they were to succeed in building a united front against King Elgron, it would require more than just words. They would need to earn each other's trust, something he couldn't help but feel confident about achieving.

As they discussed the details of their plan, Mr. Brogath found himself becoming increasingly aware of his own persuasive abilities. Time and again, he was able to steer the conversation in the right direction, somehow winning Roth over to his point of view with ease. Almost accidentally, at times.

"Perhaps I have a knack for diplomacy," Mr. Brogath mused internally, intrigued by the ease with which he was able to sway the cautious wizard. This newfound talent only fueled his determination to bridge the gap between

Roth and the rebel faction, for the sake of both the magic users and the oppressed citizens of the kingdom.

"Remember," Roth warned, his eyes narrowing as he studied Mr. Brogath intently, "if they betray us, we won't hesitate to sever ties and defend ourselves. I'll remind you that wizards have long lives and longer memories."

"Of course," Mr. Brogath assured him, meeting Roth's gaze with unwavering sincerity. "My intentions are nothing but honorable. Together, we have a chance to change the world for the better."

With a final nod of agreement, Roth extended his hand, and Mr. Brogath grasped it firmly, sealing their tentative pact. The night air grew colder as the first stars appeared in the sky, and both knew that the road ahead would be fraught with challenges.

As Mr. Brogath prepared to leave the wizard's tower, he couldn't help but ponder over his recent discovery of his persuasive talents. As he began to descend the worn stone steps, he wondered if this ability was something he'd always had, locked away deep within him, or if it had been a skill honed through the trials he'd faced thus far.

"Roth," he called out, pausing on the staircase and turning back towards the wizened mage. "May I ask you one last question before I go?"

"Of course," Roth replied, leaning against his staff with a weary expression. "What's on your mind?"

"Throughout our conversation and others, I've noticed that I seem to have a... gift for persuasion," Mr. Brogath began, rubbing the back of his neck sheepishly. "I can't help but wonder if this is some form of magical ability or simply a skill I've developed in my past."

Roth tilted his head, his eyes scrutinizing Mr. Brogath intently. After a moment of silence, he spoke. "I cannot sense any magic in you like I can with other wizards. However, there is something about you that is certainly not normal. It's almost otherworldly, like it did not originate from these lands."

"Otherworldly?" Mr. Brogath echoed, his heart pounding as an uneasy sensation washed over him. What could this mean? And why couldn't he remember anything about his past that might explain it?

"Unfortunately, I can't offer any more insight than that," Roth admitted, his brow furrowing. "But whatever this ability is, it seems to be uniquely yours, and I'm relieved you're using it for good. Whatever you are, you are neither human, nor truly raccoon. You are also not a wizard as I know one to be. Though I'd wager that if you have some kind of power of influence, no one would be the wiser to it."

"Thank you," Mr. Brogath said, swallowing hard as he grappled with this newfound revelation. Though it didn't provide any answers about his identity or past, it at least confirmed that there was something extraordinary about him. He could only hope that, in time, he would learn the truth behind it.

"Take care, Mr. Brogath," Roth said, offering a small, genuine smile. "And remember, we're counting on you to make this alliance work."

"I won't let you down," Mr. Brogath promised, his resolve strengthening as he turned and continued down the stairs, each step echoing through the dimly lit tower.

As he stepped out into the crisp night air, Mr. Brogath took a deep breath, steeling himself for the journey ahead. There was much at stake, and the weight of responsibility rested heavily on his shoulders. But with each stride, he felt more certain of his path and the role he was meant to play in shaping the destiny of their world.

With Roth's words still fresh in his mind, Mr. Brogath set off towards the rebel camp, determined to convince Galen that an alliance with the wizards was exactly what they needed to defeat King Elgron and bring peace to their troubled kingdom.

CHAPTER NINE

Mr. Brogath stumbled into the rebel camp, his fur matted and tangled with leaves, twigs, and dirt. He had been away for days, seeking out Roth, the reclusive wizard everyone called "evil" but who Mr. Brogath believed might be their last hope against King Elgron. The raccoon looked around, his eyes adjusting to the chaos that seemed to have been stoked even further in his absence.

"Ah, Mr. Brogath!" bellowed Galen, his booming voice cutting through the cacophony of arguments and clashing steel. "You've returned! And not a moment too soon, it seems."

"Indeed," Mr. Brogath replied, trying to regain his composure. "I bring news from Roth, the wizard himself. He's agreed to join our cause."

"Really?" Galen raised an eyebrow skeptically. "That's... unexpected."

"Desperate times call for desperate measures," Mr. Brogath muttered, glancing at the tense faces of the rebels.

"Perhaps there's something to that," Galen conceded. "However, we have more pressing matters at the moment.

I've made my final decision. We will attack the village loyal to King Elgron. It's time to send him a message."

"You still want to attack the village?" Mr. Brogath asked, taken aback. "But these are innocent people!"

"For now, they're innocent. Tomorrow? Sometimes sacrifices must be made." Galen's jaw clenched as he met Mr. Brogath's gaze. "We can't afford to lose any more ground to Elgron. Far more than a single village is at stake."

Mr. Brogath surveyed the divided rebels, his heart sinking. The disagreement over Galen's proposed attack had only grown worse while he was away, now threatening to tear the rebellion apart. They were supposed to be fighting against tyranny, not each other.

"Please reconsider," Mr. Brogath pleaded. "There must be another way."

"Enough!" Galen snapped, his patience wearing thin. "We don't have time for this anymore. We need to act now!"

"Is this what you've become?" Mr. Brogath asked softly, his voice barely audible over the rising din of voices and clanging metal. "This is the decision King Elgron would make in your shoes. How are you any better than the king you fight against?"

"Watch your words, raccoon," Galen warned, a dangerous edge to his voice.

"Wait just a moment, Galen," Rila interjected. Her eyes were filled with uncertainty, but her stance held steady. "We aren't done discussing this."

"This is war!" Galen growled, frustration boiling over. "And if you can't handle it, then maybe you should've stayed home."

"I don't have a home, Galen. My whole family is gone. Same as yours. It's the same for most of the others here," Rila replied, her tone icy. "But perhaps there's a better way for us to resolve this," she said, letting her hand rest on the hilt of her sword.

"Such as?" Galen challenged, folding his arms across his chest.

"Let's put it to a vote," suggested Mr. Brogath, hoping to diffuse the situation. "That way, everyone's voice will be heard."

Galen's face was a grim mask as he stood before the gathered rebels. The firelight danced across their eager, angry faces, casting eerie shadows on the forest floor. Among them, Rila stared at Galen with a mixture of disbelief and frustration, her arms crossed defensively over her chest.

"Enough!" Galen barked, his voice carrying through the camp. "The decision has been made. We strike the village at dawn. Prepare yourselves."

"Wait!" Rila shouted, stepping forward. "You can't just ignore our objections like they don't matter!"

"Rila," Mr. Brogath said in an undertone, placing a paw on her shoulder, "perhaps there's another way we can convince-"

"No," she snapped, brushing his paw away. "I've done everything I can to reason with him, but it's clear he won't listen and we're out of time." She turned back to Galen, her eyes blazing with determination. "If you can't see that attacking innocent villagers is a mistake, then maybe you shouldn't be leading us."

Galen's eyes narrowed dangerously. He looked around at the other rebels, some nodding in agreement with Rila, others shifting uncomfortably, unsure where their loyalties lay. His mind raced, trying to find a way to maintain control over the situation without causing an all-out rebellion within the ranks.

"Rila," he began, his voice low and measured, "I understand your concerns. But we cannot afford to hesitate any longer. This is our chance to deal a significant blow to King Elgron's plans by cutting off his contact with this area."

"By attacking innocents?" Rila shot back, her voice trembling with anger. "That goes against everything we stand for!"

"Every war has its casualties, Rila," Galen replied, though the weight of her words settled heavily in his heart. "I do not relish the thought, but it's a necessary sacrifice."

"Enough with your words!" Rila shouted, her voice echoing through the trees. "If you won't listen to reason, then we'll resolve this another way, Galen! A duel, here and now, to decide who should lead the rebellion! That's the rule we set to resolve these kinds of stalemates, after all."

Silence descended upon the camp like a suffocating blanket. Even the crackling fire seemed to quieten as the rebels stared at Rila in disbelief. Mr. Brogath looked from Rila to Galen, his heart pounding in his chest. He knew that if Rila and Galen fought, it could potentially make things even worse.

"Rila," he whispered urgently, "are you sure about this?"

"Absolutely," she replied, her gaze locked on Galen, who regarded her with a mixture of surprise and admiration. For the first time, he seemed to hear her words clearly.

"Very well," Galen said finally, his voice cold and hard as steel. "A duel it is, but know this: If you lose, you will abide by my decision without question."

"Agreed," Rila responded, her voice steady despite the fear that gripped her heart. "And if I win, we delay the attack and explore other options."

"Fine," Galen growled, unsheathing his sword with a metallic rasp and eying the much smaller woman up and down. "I'll try not to hurt you, but I can't make any promises."

As the two combatants squared off, Mr. Brogath couldn't help but feel a sense of unease settle over him. The fate of the rebellion hung in the balance, and there was no way to tell what the outcome would be. But one thing was certain: things were about to change, and not everyone would be happy with the result.

The crackling fires cast long shadows across the makeshift dueling ring. Rila's heart pounded in her chest as she gripped her curved blade, the cold metal reassuring against her calloused fingers. Galen towered over her, his heavy broadsword gleaming in the fading light. The rebels formed a tense circle around them, their faces etched with worry and anticipation.

"Begin!" shouted Galen, his voice even and confident.

He lunged forward, his sword slicing through the air like a guillotine. Rila sidestepped the blow, her smaller frame serving as an advantage in evading his attacks. Though it would not do her any favors if she tried to block them. She could feel the eyes of the rebels on her, weighing her worth. Doubt gnawed at the edges of her thoughts, but she pushed it away, focusing on her opponent.

"Is that all you've got?" Galen taunted, a confident smile dancing on his lips. "Remember that you can yield at any point."

Rila gritted her teeth, refusing to rise to his bait. Instead, she let her training take over, her body moving with fluid grace as she parried, dodged, and struck. She never met his strength with strength. Each exchange revealed small openings in Galen's defense, which Rila exploited with ruthless efficiency. All of her successful attacks were small, shallow cuts, but they quickly began to add up, with most of the damage being to Galen's ego. And without a single injury of her own.

The rebels watched, breathless, as the dance of steel continued. Their once fearless leader was beginning to slow, sweat beading on his brow and his movements growing more labored. Blood trickled from dozens of wounds. Rila's relentless assault chipped away at his stamina, her lighter blade darting in and out like a viper, curving and rolling through the air like an unpredictable leaf lazily riding a summer breeze. It slowly became clear to him that it wasn't he who was toying with his opponent, but the other way around.

"Come on, Galen," Rila hissed, her voice barely audible above the clash of swords. Her chest barely moved. She wasn't even winded. "Show me what you're made of. Remember, you can yield at any time."

Her words seemed to ignite a spark within him, and for a moment, Galen rallied, his sword swinging with renewed vigor. He hoped to gamble on his massive power advantage and win in a single strike, if only he could land one. If he could, the duel would perhaps be over in that single blow.

But that hope was short-lived. A wild swing left him off-balance, and Rila seized the opportunity. With a swift, precise motion, she disarmed him. His sword clattered to the ground, and Galen stumbled back.

"Yield," Rila demanded, her blade pressed against his throat.

"I yield," he croaked, the fight draining from his eyes, replaced by a new spark that seemed to Mr. Brogath almost like the look of a proud father.

A murmur of disbelief rippled through the crowd. Some rebels accused Rila of cheating; others were awestruck by her victory. Amidst the chaos, Galen raised his hand for silence.

"Listen!" he bellowed, his voice carrying across the clearing. "I stand before you a defeated man. Rila bested me fair and square, and I will support her as our new leader. My final order is that you do the same."

The tension in the air began to dissipate as murmurs of agreement echoed amongst the rebels. Rila's heart swelled with pride and relief, but she knew that this was only the beginning. Their true battle still lay ahead, and they would need every ounce of strength and unity to face it.

"Well then," she said, turning to address the gathered rebels, "I think it's time we heard from our friend here. Mr. Brogath, why have you returned to our camp?"

"Ah, yes," Mr. Brogath replied, standing on his hind legs and brushing himself off. "I met with the wizard, Roth."

"Roth?" Galen interjected, furrowing his brow. "The one they call The Evil Wizard?"

"Indeed," Mr. Brogath continued. "However, I've discovered that he is misunderstood. Wizards are actively hunted, with their only crime being refusing to serve King Elgron. He has offered to join forces with us."

A wave of disbelief and skepticism washed over the crowd.

"Join forces with an evil wizard?" one rebel spat. "Are you mad?"

"Look, I know it sounds crazy," Rila admitted, her voice steady and commanding. "But we must consider all our options. We can't afford to reject potential allies based on hearsay and rumors."

"Rila's right," Galen chimed in. "It's likely those rumors were started by King Elgron himself to turn us against each other. Remember, the wizard attacked Elgron's castle not long ago. They're clearly not on the same side."

"Besides," Rila added, "we could use some powerful magic on our side for once."

After a tense moment, the rebels began to nod in agreement, the weight of their decision settling upon them.

"Very well," Rila announced. "We'll join forces with the wizard, Roth. Let's just hope this alliance proves fruitful."

As if on cue, a crow cawed overhead, black wings slicing through the sky before disappearing into the distance.

"Ah, there goes our messenger," Mr. Brogath muttered with a hint of amusement. "Perhaps it's time we prepared for the next phase of our fight."

"Indeed," Rila said, determination etched on her face.

Their conversation was interrupted by a wounded man stumbling into the camp, his eyes wide with fear and urgency. In his hands, he clutched a sealed parchment.

"I'm so sorry, Galen. They discovered Seraphine and... She's..." He clutched at his wounds, tears streaming down his cheeks. "Commander Thorne has sent an invitation," he panted. "He requests a meeting with the rebel leadership."

The rebels exchanged wary glances, suspicion gnawing at their newfound unity. Two of the men rushed forward, helping the messenger inside. He was one of Seraphine's men.

"That's one of our scouts who was captured nearly a week ago," Galen said, his voice laced with sorrow. "I feared the worst when I hadn't heard from them but... Oh Seraphine, you deserved so much better. At least someone made it out alive."

"My heart is glad to see he survived, but it seems like a trap to me," another rebel whispered. "However he discovered it, Elgron knows where we are now."

"Agreed," another chimed in.

"Regardless," Rila declared, stepping forward, "I must go. If Elgron knows our location, we can't afford to delay any longer."

"Rila, are you sure? This isn't an invitation, but a threat. He is telling us he knows where we are, and can crush us at any time," Galen said, concern creeping into his voice. "Let me go. I'll be who he's expecting anyway. You are our leader now. If someone should walk into certain death, let it be me."

"No," she replied, her resolve unwavering. "I'll face whatever comes my way, and so will the rest of us. For now, let's prepare for the fight ahead. Come morning, I will meet Commander Thorne face to face and show him we aren't afraid."

With that, Rila strode toward the edge of the camp, her thoughts racing as she contemplated the storm that was brewing on the horizon.

Under the cloak of darkness, Mr. Brogath's small raccoon form scurried through the shadows of the rebel camp, his tiny heart pounding in his chest. The weight of Rila's safety bore heavily on him, and he knew he had to meet with Commander Thorne himself. He couldn't let her walk into a trap.

"Think fast, Mr. Brogath," he muttered under his breath, slipping past a dozing guard. "You've got one shot at this. Don't botch it."

As he darted through the quiet moonlit woods, he tried to summon what little powers of persuasion he might possess. It was a gamble, but he'd been adapting well so far.

Perhaps there was more hidden within him than he realized.

"Convince Thorne..." he whispered, barely audible even to himself. "There must be some way..."

Upon reaching the designated meeting spot – a dilapidated courtyard half-consumed by nature's relentless grasp – Mr. Brogath hesitated for a moment, sensing something amiss. But the urgency of his mission propelled him forward.

"Commander Thorne?" he called out cautiously, his voice wavering. "It's Mr. Brogath. I'm here to talk."

From the shadows, Commander Thorne emerged, his face betraying no emotion. "So you are," he replied, a hint of curiosity in his tone. "But what brings you here instead of Galen?"

"Don't concern yourself with that," Mr. Brogath said, his eyes locked on Thorne's. "I hope to convince you that we can find a peaceful solution to our conflict."

"Is that so?" Thorne asked, raising an eyebrow.

"Indeed," Mr. Brogath continued, his voice gaining strength. "We both know King Elgron is the true enemy here. His tyranny oppresses us all. If we unite against him, we can bring about real change for the better. Without his commander to support him, he will have no one. The battle can end without a single drop of blood being shed. Don't you also want to do what's best for the people?"

For a moment, Thorne's eyes betrayed emotion and he seemed to consider his words, but then he stepped back, revealing a group of soldiers hiding in the shadows. Their weapons were drawn and pointed at Mr. Brogath, who had been expecting them.

"An admirable sentiment, raccoon," Thorne said coldly as the soldiers closed in, his voice betraying a tinge of regret.

"But my loyalty is to King Elgron. You've made a grave mistake coming here alone."

"Have I?" Mr. Brogath said, trying to appear confident while panic clawed at his insides like a desperate animal. "Or is there still hope for us after all? Maybe there's more to your story than being a blind follower, Thorne. It's never too late to do the right thing."

As the soldiers surrounded him, Mr. Brogath took one final look around, desperately searching for an escape, a plan, anything. But there was nothing – only the encroaching darkness and the ominous caw of a crow, its black wings slicing through the night as it vanished from sight.

CHAPTER TEN

Roth and three other wizards arrived at the rebel camp, carried by the morning sun. Their robes billowed around them like storm clouds, their eyes gleaming with knowledge and power. Galen felt a shiver of apprehension run down his spine. He had never seen so many wizards gathered in one place, and he couldn't help but feel that it was an omen of something terrible to come.

"My new friends," Roth began, his voice deep and resonant, "I am Roth, a wizard, and I bring news of Mr. Brogath's capture." The rebels exchanged uneasy glances, a ripple of murmurs spreading through the crowd. Rila gripped her sword tightly, her knuckles turning white. The words only confirmed what she already knew.

"Tell us what happened," Galen demanded, anxiety gnawing at him like a persistent rat.

"Commander Thorne laid a trap," Roth explained, his expression solemn. "It was intended to ensnare the rebel leader and draw out the remaining rebels to be slaughtered or force their quick surrender. The trap was meant for you, Galen."

The revelation struck Galen like a blow to the chest. Guilt weighed heavy on his shoulders, threatening to crush him beneath its suffocating embrace. Mr. Brogath, the curious raccoon who had put so much on the line for their rebellion, was now in the clutches of their enemy because of him. Because of his own weakness, his inability to see the danger lurking in the shadows. His own arrogance.

"Roth," Rila spoke up, her voice unsteady. "What do you suggest?"

"First, we must accept responsibility for our actions," Roth replied, his gaze piercing into each of them. "We have all played a part in Mr. Brogath's capture, whether directly or indirectly. Myself included. He made me realize we have become too hesitant to act in our old age."

Galen saw the guilt mirrored in Rila's eyes, and he knew that she too bore the weight of their failure. They had both been so focused on their own struggles that they had failed to protect their new friend.

"Second," Roth continued, "we must choose our next move carefully, but quickly. Time is running out, but we cannot afford any missteps."

"Whatever it takes, we'll get him back," Galen vowed.

"Indeed," Roth agreed, a hint of a smile touching his lips. "We will face many challenges in the hours ahead, but together, with our combined strength, we will overcome them. Just as Mr. Brogath knew we would."

Rila surveyed the scene before them, her heart heavy with the weight of responsibility. They stood at the edge of a dense forest, the castle looming in the distance like a dark sentinel. The wind whispered through the trees, carrying the scent of damp earth and the threat of impending violence.

"Alright," Roth said, breaking the silence. "We cannot wait any longer. We need a quick plan."

The rebel leaders and wizards huddled together, their voices low as they discussed their strategy. Galen's thoughts raced, his fingers tracing the hilt of his sword.

"King Elgron will be expecting us," Rila pointed out, her brow furrowed with concern. "He knows we're coming for Mr. Brogath."

"True," Roth agreed. "But he won't be expecting your little surprise." The wizard gestured to himself and his three fellow mages. "They've never seen the likes of us before, fighting together. I was alone the last time I attacked. Few times in history have four mages combined their power in a single battle. Although we are old now, our magic is just as strong as it was when we were young. Perhaps stronger. But we are frail and vulnerable. We will need your protection while we focus on attacking."

Galen's pulse quickened at the thought of their combined strength. With the wizards' help, they had a real chance at rescuing Mr. Brogath. Not only that, but this was perhaps their best chance to end King Elgron's tyranny once and for all. Today could be the day.

"Here's what we'll do," Roth continued. "As leaders, Rila and I will lead a frontal assault on the castle gates. While we distract King Elgron's forces, the rest of you will split into two teams and breach the walls from either side."

"Once inside," another wizard interjected, "we'll converge on the dungeon where Mr. Brogath is being held. We free him and make our escape."

"Simple enough," Galen muttered, though he knew nothing about this rescue mission would be easy.

Rila shook her head. "No. There will be no retreat. This

is our best chance to end King Elgron's rule, and it's a chance we should take."

Roth smiled. "Well said. Though time is of the essence," he warned. "We should strike at nightfall. They will not realize there are wizards among you until it is too late. By day, they may easily target us with their arrows."

As dusk settled over the land, casting eerie shadows across the castle grounds, the rebels and wizards put their plan into action. Rila and Roth led the charge. Lightning crackled across the sky, illuminating the fierce determination in their eyes.

Galen's group moved swiftly and silently, scaling the castle walls with the aid of grapples and ropes. His heart pounded in his chest as he hoisted himself over the edge, adrenaline coursing through his veins.

"Stick to the plan," Galen whispered to his team, his voice barely audible above the din of battle. "Everyone is counting on us."

They slipped through the shadows, avoiding patrolling guards and making their way toward the dungeon. The other wizards demonstrated their prowess, casting spells that sent enemy soldiers flying or rendered them unconscious.

As they neared the entrance to the dungeon, Galen spotted the second rebel group converging on their position. They exchanged grim nods, knowing the most dangerous part of their mission still lay ahead.

"Ready?" Roth asked, his eyes alight with a fierce intensity. The rebels and wizards steeled themselves, preparing for the final push.

"Let's get Brogath back," Galen replied, his voice resolute.

With a battle cry, they stormed the castle on their way to the dungeon, their combined strength a force to be reckoned with. Swords clashed and magic flared as they engaged King Elgron's soldiers, determined to free their friend and restore balance to their world.

***

The cold, damp air of the dungeon seemed to seep into Mr. Brogath's very bones as he was led down the narrow, torchlit corridor. The clanking of the chains that bound him echoed off the stone walls, a haunting reminder of his dire situation. He tried not to think about the fate that awaited him, focusing instead on the details of his surroundings: the moss growing between the stones, the oily black smoke that curled from each flickering torch.

"Move it, vermin!" one of the guards snapped, prodding Mr. Brogath with the butt of his spear.

He stumbled forward, catching himself on the wall before resuming his shuffling pace. They reached a heavy wooden door, its surface marred by gouges and scratches. The guard fumbled with a set of keys, finally unlocking the door and shoving Mr. Brogath inside.

"Enjoy your stay," the guard sneered, slamming the door shut behind him.

Mr. Brogath surveyed his new prison. The cell was small and windowless, little more than a hole in the ground. A thin layer of moldy straw covered the floor, and rusty shackles hung from the walls. In one corner, a bucket served as a makeshift toilet. It was clear that comfort was not a priority in King Elgron's all-too-familiar dungeon.

His heart raced as the reality of his situation began to sink in. "I can't believe I'm here again," he thought, his mind racing with memories of his friends and the battles they'd fought together. "How could I have let them down? What if I never see them again?"

As if in answer to his thoughts, the door creaked open once more. Mr. Brogath's eyes widened in shock as King Elgron himself strode into the cell, flanked by two guards who quickly retreated, leaving the king alone with his prisoner.

"Ah, Mr. Brogath," King Elgron said with a thin-lipped smile, his eyes glittering like ice. "I've been looking forward to seeing you again."

"Your Majesty," Mr. Brogath spat.

"You're here because I believe you possess something I want – something that will make me more powerful than anyone could ever imagine."

"Powerful?" Mr. Brogath thought, an uneasy feeling settling in his stomach. What could the king possibly want from him? And what did it have to do with power?

"Allow me to explain," King Elgron continued, his voice dripping with arrogance. "I am not just a ruler – I am a wizard, one who has spent countless years honing my skills and gathering knowledge. I have dedicated my life to the pursuit of power, and I will stop at nothing to claim what is rightfully mine."

"Y-you're a wizard?" Mr. Brogath stuttered, his heart pounding even harder now. This changed everything. Did Roth even know about this?

"Indeed," the king replied, a wicked grin stretching across his face. "And it is my belief that you possess a rare and dangerous magic – one that I can take for myself. The only obstacle standing in my way is you."

As King Elgron's words hung heavy in the air, Mr. Brogath felt a new resolve begin to take hold. He would not let this tyrant steal whatever power he might hold. He would fight, with every ounce of strength he had left. Just like Seraphine did for him.

"Elgron," he said, lifting his chin in defiance, "you may have me chained and locked away, but you will never break me. If I do have any power, it will never be yours."

The king's eyes narrowed, but his smile never wavered. "We shall see, Mr. Brogath," he hissed, turning on his heel and leaving the cell. "We shall see."

The air in the dungeon grew colder, as if the very stones around Mr. Brogath were closing in on him. King Elgron stood in the shadows, his eyes gleaming with predatory intent. "Has it never occurred to you that there is no such thing in our lands as a talking raccoon? I'm aware of every shred of magic in this land, but you suddenly appeared one day out of nowhere. You may not know it yet, but I believe you possess a magic so potent that it could reshape this world," he said, his voice low and threatening.

"Magic?" Mr. Brogath asked, confusion lacing his words. "But I'm just... I don't even know who or what I am, even if what you say is true."

"Your ignorance will be your undoing," the king said dismissively. "I have devised a ritual, one that will extract the magic from within you and transfer it to me. Soon, I will possess the power to bend this realm to my will."

Mr. Brogath's breath caught in his throat at the thought of such a terrible fate. He looked down at his raccoon paws and clenched them into small fists. "You're wrong," he whispered, defiance rising within him. "You won't succeed."

"Your bravado is amusing," King Elgron sneered. "But ultimately pointless."

Outside the castle walls, the battle between the rebels, mages, and King Elgron's forces rallied their defense. Roth led the charge, his powerful spells ripping through the air like lightning bolts, while Galen and Rila fought alongside their fellow rebels, swords clashing with those of the enemy.

"Push forward!" Roth roared, conjuring a swirling vortex of wind that sent several of the king's soldiers flying. "We must reach the dungeon!"

"Stay close to Roth!" Galen shouted to Rila, slicing through a soldier who tried to block their path. "He's our best chance of getting to Mr. Brogath, and there is no one more capable than you to protect him!"

As they fought their way deeper into the castle grounds, their momentum grew. The rebels and wizards gained ground, forcing King Elgron's forces to retreat deeper in.

"Keep pressing!" Roth commanded, his eyes focused on the looming castle. "We're almost there!"

Inside the dungeon, Mr. Brogath's thoughts raced, searching for any means of escape. He knew he had to find a way out, a way to fight back against the king's dark intentions. But how?

"Perhaps I do have magic," he thought, desperation clawing at him. "But if I do, how can I unlock it? How can I use it to save myself – and this world?"

King Elgron studied Mr. Brogath with a cold, calculating gaze. "Your defiance will be short-lived," he warned, stepping closer to the cell bars. "The ritual will begin soon. And when it is complete, your power will be mine."

"Never," Mr. Brogath whispered, his voice trembling as much from fear as determination. "I'll find a way to stop you."

"Such confidence," King Elgron said, a cruel smile twisting his lips. "Savor it while you can, for soon it will be nothing more than a memory."

As the battle raged on outside the castle walls, Mr. Brogath steeled himself for the coming night, knowing that his only hope lay in discovering the hidden depths of his own power – whatever they might be – and using them to thwart the king's sinister plans.

***

The clash of steel against steel rang through the air, punctuated by the cries of pain and fury from both sides as the battle outside the castle walls surged on. Rebels and wizards fought side by side, their faces etched with determination and desperation, knowing that every moment counted in their struggle to save Mr. Brogath.

A rebel soldier's anguished scream tore through the air as he fell, his lifeblood staining the ground beneath him. The surrounding area bore the scars of the conflict – the once-pristine grass now trampled and muddied, the castle walls pockmarked with spells that had gone awry, and the bodies of the fallen, a grim testament to the cost of their defiance against King Elgron. Many buildings were smashed to the ground. It was no wonder the wizards hesitated to use their power.

"We're almost there!" Roth bellowed over the cacophony, rallying the rebels and casting powerful spells that sent the king's forces reeling. But for every enemy they struck down, it seemed another took their place, the relentless tide of King Elgron's soldiers threatening to overwhelm them in their swarm.

Inside the dungeon, Mr. Brogath paced nervously within his cell, his heart pounding in his chest as he listened to the distant echoes of battle. He clenched his fists, feeling helpless and trapped, desperate to aid his friends and foil King Elgron's plans.

"Can you hear the sound of your allies' demise?" King Elgron taunted, his voice cold and malicious as he stood just outside the cell bars. "Soon, there will be no one left to save you, little raccoon. Your power will be mine, and I will crush whatever is left of their forces personally. If anything remains at all."

"Your hunger for power will be your downfall," Mr. Brogath spat back, his eyes blazing with defiance. "You underestimate the determination of those who oppose you."

"Determination is nothing without strength," King Elgron sneered.

"Then you've already lost," Mr. Brogath countered, his voice filled with resolve. "Even if you take my power, you'll never break their spirits."

King Elgron scoffed at the notion before turning away to prepare, leaving Mr. Brogath to stew in his own thoughts, his heart aching for the friends who fought on his behalf.

"Is this truly all I can do?" he wondered, despair gnawing at him. "Must I simply wait while others risk everything for me?"

As the sounds of battle raged on, Mr. Brogath knew that time was running out. With each beat of his heart, another precious moment slipped away, bringing him closer to the fateful confrontation with King Elgron and the ritual that threatened to steal his very essence. His only hope lay in finding a way to unlock whatever hidden power he possessed and turn it against the king — but with every fiber of his being, he prayed that it would be enough.

Commander Thorne's boots echoed against the cold stone floor of the dungeon as he led his main force, including the twelve elite assassins known as the Black Cloaks, through the dimly lit corridors. The air was heavy with the scent of damp earth and the faintly acrid tang of blood from the ongoing battle above. His heart pounded in his chest, torn between duty and doubt, as he glanced over his shoulder at the determined faces of his men.

"Secure the entrance!" he barked, gritting his teeth as the sound of spells and steel clashed above them. The Black Cloaks moved swiftly into formation, barricading the dungeon doors with a combination of brute force and years of training. Thorne knew that even the wizards and rebels would be hard-pressed to breach such a barrier, buying precious time for King Elgron.

"Your Majesty," Thorne called out, urgency threading through his voice. "The situation is dire; we must focus on bolstering our defenses. If we don't retreat, our soldiers will be slaughtered for nothing."

King Elgron, however, paid no heed to Thorne's words. Instead, his eyes were locked onto Mr. Brogath, who paced the confines of his cell like the caged animal he was. The king strode forward, letting himself in, the heavy iron door slamming shut behind him, leaving him trapped within the cell alongside his captive. Thorne and his troops could only watch, anxiety ripping through them.

"Enough of your prattling, Thorne!" King Elgron snapped, his gaze never wavering from the raccoon before him. "I have more pressing matters to attend to. It is a soldier's duty to die for his king, after all. Just slow them down."

Inside the cell, Mr. Brogath's mind raced, panic and despair threatening to overwhelm him. He searched for a weakness, a hidden reserve of power that might turn the tide in their favor. But as he met the king's cold, calculating stare, he couldn't help but wonder if this truly was the end.

"Your Majesty, please," Thorne implored, desperation seeping into his voice as he watched his king ignore the chaos unfolding around them. "The rebels and wizards are gaining ground. Nothing short of a god could defeat four wizards. We must focus on our defenses and evacuation, not on extracting power from a being that may or may not possess it."

"Silence!" King Elgron roared, finally tearing his gaze away from Mr. Brogath to glare at his commander. "Your loyalty is to me, is it not? Do as you are commanded!"

Thorne bowed his head, swallowing the bitter taste of anger and frustration that threatened to choke him. "As you wish, Your Majesty," he murmured, gritting his teeth as he turned to address his troops. The battle raged on above them, the sounds of destruction and death seeping through the dungeon walls like a haunting melody.

"Prepare for their arrival," Thorne ordered, struggling to keep the tremor of fear from his voice. "If the king will not evacuate, we must hold the line, no matter the cost."

CHAPTER ELEVEN

The dank prison cell was suffused with an eerie silence, broken only by the occasional whimper of a desperate inmate. The walls were slick with moisture and mottled with mold, casting grotesque shadows in the dim light. King Elgron stood before Mr. Brogath with a sinister smile creeping across his face, his eyes glinting with malevolent intent.

"Mr. Brogath," he began, his voice cold as ice, "You may be a mere raccoon now, but I know there is more to you than meets the eye."

Mr. Brogath chittered nervously, his bushy tail twitching involuntarily as he eyed the imposing figure of the king. He knew not what powers this man spoke of, nor did he understand how he might possess them. All he could do was brace himself for whatever came next.

With a swift motion, King Elgron produced an ancient-looking tome from his robes and flipped through its brittle pages until he found the passage he sought. His eyes darted back and forth as he read, then he began to chant in a language that seemed as old as time itself. The air crackled with energy as the words echoed through the chamber, like the sudden hush before a thunderstorm.

As the ritual unfolded, Mr. Brogath felt an invisible force pulling at him, tugging insistently at his very being. It was as if his entire essence was being drawn into a vortex, merging with something vast and incomprehensible. He struggled to maintain his grip on reality, but it was futile; the whirlwind of power enveloped him completely, and he could no longer tell where he ended and the other presence began.

King Elgron's chanting grew louder, more frantic as he sensed the ritual nearing completion. His hands trembled with excitement, his eyes wild with hunger for the power he was about to claim.

But even as King Elgron reveled in his imminent triumph, Mr. Brogath found within himself a strength he had not known he possessed. As the force that bound their minds together grew stronger, so too did his resolve to resist it.

"By the gods," Mr. Brogath thought, "I may not know who or what I am, but I cannot let this man steal from me whatever power I hold. I must fight back... somehow."

And so, with a surge of determination, Mr. Brogath pushed against the overwhelming tide that sought to strip him of his essence. He dug deep into the wellspring of his being, searching for the source of his strength, and found within himself a spark that blazed like a beacon in the darkness. Though, it was like wielding a weapon he couldn't even see. He had no grasp of how to focus it.

As the two wills clashed in a battle of minds, the room around them trembled, dust falling from the ceiling and cracks spiderwebbing across the cold stone floor. The very fabric of reality seemed to groan under the strain, and all the while, the king's chanting continued, growing more desperate and frantic by the second.

"Give in!" King Elgron snarled, his voice twisted with rage and fear. "Surrender your power to me, and perhaps I shall show you mercy!"

"Never!" Mr. Brogath's thoughts rang out defiantly, echoing through the shared mental space like a clarion call.

The clash between the two minds reached a fever pitch, each striving to overpower the other in a contest of wills that threatened to tear them both apart. And as they struggled, locked in a dance of dominance and defiance, it seemed as though the very foundations of the world would crumble beneath them.

The chanting ceased abruptly, and King Elgron's voice was replaced by a suffocating silence. The stone walls of the prison cell seemed to crumble away into nothingness, leaving Mr. Brogath floating in an infinite void.

"Where am I?" he whispered, his words echoing throughout the empty expanse.

"Ah, you've finally arrived," a deep, resonant voice replied. It belonged to none other than King Elgron, whose form shimmered into existence before Mr. Brogath. "Welcome to the deepest recesses of our minds, where our very souls have merged."

"You are a king! Can you not be satisfied with even that? Why risk so much for power you don't even need?" Mr. Brogath shouted in disbelief.

"One can never have too much power," King Elgron admitted, his eyes glittering with madness. "Now, let us see what lies hidden within you."

As if pulled by an unseen force, Mr. Brogath felt himself drawn deeper into the dark abyss, with King Elgron following close behind. They passed through a swirling vortex of memories and emotions, flashes of Mr. Brogath's life flickering like fireflies in the darkness.

"Stop this!" Mr. Brogath demanded, though he knew he was powerless against the ritual that bound their minds together. "You have no right to delve into my past!"

"Your past may hold the key to your power. Surely you want to see it too," King Elgron mused, ignoring Mr. Brogath's protests. "And thus, it shall be mine."

As they ventured further into the depths of Mr. Brogath's consciousness, the fragmented memories began to coalesce into a single, coherent vision. A revelation dawned upon Mr. Brogath as he recognized his true nature: a muse, a lesser god with abilities far beyond those of mortal men.

"Impossible..." he breathed, his eyes widening in shock. "How could I have forgotten something like this, and how did I end up here and in this state?"

"Ah, so you finally remember," King Elgron said. "See? I was right all along. You do possess great power. Oh, and what power it is. I never could've dreamed it. I will become a living god. Even the wizards will bow before me."

"Never!" Mr. Brogath snarled, the realization of his divine heritage igniting a newfound strength within him. "You may have bound our minds together, but it is you who is trapped now!"

"Bold words for a creature that has only just discovered its own identity," King Elgron taunted. "But we shall see if you can back them up with action. You've discovered your power, but you don't even remember how to wield it."

"Watch me," Mr. Brogath retorted, the fire of defiance burning brightly in his heart. As a muse, he knew that he possessed the power to inspire and shape the thoughts of others. Though he couldn't fathom how he'd ended up in this world or lost sight of his origins, he vowed to use his abilities to protect himself and those he cared for from the king's malevolent intentions. Perhaps this was the reason he was here.

"Your arrogance will be your downfall," King Elgron warned, raising a hand wreathed in dark energy. "Prepare yourself, for our battle has only just begun."

"Things have changed now. You don't stand a chance. Surrender while I'm still giving you the option," Mr. Brogath challenged, standing tall and proud against the darkness that threatened to consume him. For he was no longer a mere raccoon, but a being of immense power and potential. And he would not go down without a fight.

In this realm of merged minds, the very air seemed to

shimmer with power. King Elgron, appearing as a towering figure wreathed in shadows, loomed over Mr. Brogath, who now stood not as a raccoon but as a luminous being with an ethereal quality that defied description.

"Your powers will be mine," King Elgron declared, his voice echoing ominously through the dreamscape.

"Stop talking and take them!" Mr. Brogath shouted back, his identity as a muse surging within him like a tidal wave. With his newfound abilities came the knowledge of his unique power: the ability to influence and manipulate the thoughts of others. He didn't understand how he'd come to this world or why he'd been unaware of his true nature, but he couldn't allow King Elgron to claim his divine gifts for himself.

"Bold words for someone so lost," the king sneered, raising a hand crackling with menacing energy. "But we shall see if you can withstand my magic. It's not so different from yours, after all."

As the dark energy hurtled toward him, Mr. Brogath felt disoriented, his mind grasping for clarity amidst the chaos. The landscape around them twisted and warped, reflections of their inner turmoil. How had he, a muse, ended up here? Why couldn't he remember anything before waking up in this world? His confusion only grew as King Elgron's magic threatened to separate him from his newfound powers.

"Enough!" Mr. Brogath roared, his voice resonating with the authority of his divine power. He drew upon his own abilities, focusing on the strength that lay within him. In that moment, he understood the way he could use his gift to turn the tide of this battle.

"Feel the pain you've given to others, Elgron!" Mr.

Brogath cried, extending his paws toward the king. A brilliant light erupted from his fingertips, piercing the darkness that surrounded them.

King Elgron's eyes widened as his own thoughts and emotions began to twist and turn within him. He gasped as the very pain and suffering he had inflicted upon others were reflected back in his own mind.

"Impossible!" he spat, reeling from the power of Mr. Brogath's abilities. "You dare to use my own mind against me? Your feeble attempt at defiance will get you nowhere," Elgron sneered, his voice dripping with venom. "I've faced far greater foes than a confused little creature like yourself."

"Perhaps," Mr. Brogath replied, his voice steady despite the tumultuous emotions swirling within him. "But have you ever faced someone as terrible as yourself?"

With that, Mr. Brogath reached deeper with his newfound abilities, seeking to penetrate the king's thoughts and manipulate his thinking. As he made contact with Elgron's mind, it was like plunging into an abyss of darkness, filled with shadows and whispers of cruelty and malice. Barely a shred of empathy to be found.

King Elgron gritted his teeth, trying to push back against the invasion. His resistance was fierce, but ultimately failing. Mr. Brogath was relentless, slipping through every crack and crevice in Elgron's mental defenses, slowly winding his way around the king's twisted thoughts.

"Get out of my head!" Elgron snarled, sweat beading on his forehead as he struggled against Mr. Brogath's influence.

"Only after you face the truth," Mr. Brogath answered, undeterred by the king's anger. He dove deeper, exposing Elgron to the consequences of his many atrocities, forcing him to see the pain and suffering he had caused. He took the tiny ember of lonely empathy in Elgron's mind and gave it the fuel it needed to ignite into an inferno.

"Enough!" King Elgron cried out, his resistance crumbling under the weight of his own guilt and shame. He fell to his knees, clutching his head in his hands, as Mr. Brogath continued to sift through the darkest recesses of his mind.

"Your power is no match for mine," Mr. Brogath said softly, but with a steely determination that left no room for doubt. "This battle is over, Elgron."

King Elgron, a broken and defeated man, stared at the floor, his eyes filled with tears of regret and despair.

"See this, Elgron?" Mr. Brogath murmured, his voice a soft breeze through the king's thoughts. "A village burned to ashes. Innocent men, women, and children cast into the flames because they dared to defy your rule."

King Elgron's eyes widened as the images flooded his mind: terrified faces illuminated by firelight, children screaming for their parents, men and women making futile attempts to save their homes. He could almost feel the heat on his own skin, smell the acrid smoke that choked the air.

"Stop," he whispered, but the images continued, relentless and unforgiving.

"Or what about Seraphine?" Mr. Brogath went on, his voice gentle yet insistent. "You ordered her execution. She might've been a treasured friend to a more worthy king."

Tears stung King Elgron's eyes, hot and bitter. "I did what I had to do to maintain order! An example had to be made!"

"Is that truly what you believe?" Mr. Brogath asked, his tone laced with sadness. "Or is it something you tell yourself to justify the horrors you've inflicted?"

Elgron's heart clenched painfully, and he shook his

head, unable to speak. He couldn't escape the truth anymore; it stared him straight in the face, a mirror reflecting back the monster he'd become. A sickening realization settled in his gut: Mr. Brogath was nothing like a wizard, but rather a force beyond his comprehension.

"Who are you?" he choked out, his voice barely audible.

"Someone who sees the whole picture, Elgron," Mr. Brogath answered quietly. "And it's time for you to see it too."

As if on cue, an overwhelming wave of empathy crashed over King Elgron. The weight of his actions, the countless lives he had destroyed, pressed down on him with an unbearable force. He felt every ounce of pain and fear that he had caused, as if it were his own.

"Please," he sobbed, collapsing onto the cold stone floor. "I didn't know... I never wanted this."

"Sometimes we must face the darkest parts of ourselves," Mr. Brogath said, his voice a soothing balm against the storm of emotions raging within Elgron's soul. "You had so many opportunities to stop along the way."

King Elgron, for the first time in his life, truly understood the suffering he had caused. Faced with the enormity of his transgressions, he could do nothing but weep. His remaining mental defenses crumbled like the ancient walls of a castle under siege. The ritual that had bound his mind to Mr. Brogath's shattered, and he felt the full force of the empathy that now coursed through him. Tears streamed down his face as he fell to his knees, sobbing at the realization of the pain he had wrought upon his own people.

"Forgive me," he choked out between sobs, the words barely audible even to himself. "I was a fool."

Commander Thorne, who had been watching the scene

unfold from a distance, felt a cold knot form in his gut. All this time, he had served a ruler who seemed driven more by fear and paranoia than any true desire to protect his kingdom. He clenched his fists, anger churning within him as he thought of the men who had trusted him, the soldiers who had followed him into battle against an enemy they knew nothing about.

"Your Majesty," Commander Thorne said, his voice firm yet laced with sorrow. "I cannot stand idly by while you destroy our people for the sake of your own misguided quest for power."

King Elgron looked up, his tear-stained face contorted with anguish. "What would you have me do, Thorne? I cannot undo what has been done. You must protect me from these invaders!"

"No! I will not send these men to their deaths to save your throne. This battle is over."

With a heavy heart, Commander Thorne raised his hand high in the air, signaling his men to cease bolstering the defenses. As the soldiers paused, confusion and uncertainty rippled through their ranks.

"Men, stand down," Thorne commanded, his voice firm but tinged with regret. "Lay down your weapons and let their forces through. We are surrendering."

A murmur of dissent spread through the soldiers, their loyalty to their commander warring with their ingrained obedience to King Elgron. Thorne's gaze swept over them, meeting the eyes of each man he had trained and fought beside for years.

"Trust me, my brothers," he implored. "Most of you have someone waiting for you at home, and I'll not see you throw your life away for nothing. Our duty should be first to our people. Our king has long since lost his way, and we must find our own."

One by one, the soldiers hesitantly lowered their weapons, their expressions a mix of relief and trepidation. Thorne knew that this decision would change everything for them – and for him – but it was a choice that had to be made.

"Rila!" Thorne called out, stepping forward and raising his voice above the clamor. "I come to you in surrender on behalf of our troops. We wish to end this bloodshed."

The young rebel woman emerged through the towering dungeon doors, her sword still in hand but her eyes alight with a glimmer of hope. She approached Thorne slowly, studying him intently as if trying to understand the truth behind his words.

"Is this a trick, Thorne?" she asked cautiously, her grip tightening on her weapon.

Thorne shook his head, his eyes never leaving hers. "No trick, Rila. I have accepted the truth of our king, and I cannot in good conscience continue to serve him. My men and I offer our surrender – and our allegiance, if you will have us. We have much to make up for."

He could feel the weight of his men's eyes upon him, their trust in him both a burden and an honor. Thorne knew that he was taking a risk by putting their lives in Rila's hands, but it was a risk he had to take for the sake of their kingdom.

"Very well," Rila said finally, her voice steady and resolute. "I accept your surrender, Commander Thorne. Rather than imprison you and your men, I'll take you up on that offer to make things right. Many strong hands will be needed to rebuild."

"Understood," Thorne replied, nodding solemnly as he

looked back toward his men. "We are with you, Rila. We are ready to make amends, whatever the cost."

With that, the remnants of the once-proud army stood down, their banners lowered in submission as they faced the unknown future before them. In the hushed silence that followed, many of the men heaved a great sigh of relief, glad the years of horror had finally come to an end.

CHAPTER TWELVE

Where sorrow and despair had reigned, laughter and determination now filled the air. The people worked side by side with renewed vigor, their spirits lifted by the fall of King Elgron and the end of wizard persecution.

Mr. Brogath gazed upon the bustling scene before him. No longer burdened by the heavy weight of uncertainty, he'd grown to accept his extended stay in this world that he now knew wasn't his own.

"Pass me that stone, would you?" called out a burly man as he wiped sweat from his brow.

"Of course!" Mr. Brogath replied, using his nimble paws to lift a hefty block of masonry. He marveled at the strength he possessed in this strange form, feeling a sense of pride as he contributed to the reconstruction efforts.

"Thanks, little guy," the man said, nodding appreciatively. "You're stronger than you look."

Mr. Brogath's whiskers twitched in amusement. "I suppose I am," he agreed thoughtfully. As he continued to work, he couldn't help but feel an odd connection to the people around him. Though he still struggled to recall the entirety of his past, he felt as if he belonged among them. He no longer cared to find out more.

"Mr. Brogath, could you help me lift this beam?" asked a young woman, struggling under its weight.

"Sure thing!" he responded, scampering over to assist her. As they hoisted the beam into place, she smiled gratefully at him.

"Thank you," she said sincerely. "Your kindness means the world to us."

"Happy to help," Mr. Brogath replied, his heart swelling with a warmth that transcended mere physical labor. He realized he could still forge a new path for himself in this world – one filled with kindness and purpose.

As the day wore on, Mr. Brogath's thoughts turned to The Bearded Fool, the enigmatic figure who had observed him from the shadows throughout his journey. What role did this mysterious individual play in his life? Who was he, really?

"Hey, Mr. Brogath!" shouted the burly man, interrupting his musings. "Come join us for dinner!"

"Sounds good," Mr. Brogath replied, shaking off his questions for now. He would find answers in due time, but for now, he had a newfound sense of belonging among these resilient people, who had welcomed him into their hearts and homes.

And so, beneath the fading sunlight, Mr. Brogath feasted with his newfound friends, laughter echoing through the air as they shared tales of their hardships and triumphs. Though darkness still lingered at the edges of his past, the muse began to understand that there was hope even in the most desperate of times. With each passing day, he drew closer to discovering the truth about his identity, and he vowed to embrace it with open arms, whatever it may be.

Sunlight filtered through the canopy of trees, dappling the earth in a kaleidoscope of warm hues. The air was filled with the sound of hammering and laughter, as the kingdom's citizens worked together to rebuild their world after King Elgron's defeat.

Amidst this bustling scene, Mr. Brogath rolled up his sleeves and adjusted his tool belt. As he drove nails into wooden beams, sweat glistened on his brow, and satisfaction swelled within him. He had found purpose in helping to mend the fractured kingdom, and each day brought him closer to understanding who he truly was.

"Alright, that's enough for today," Mr. Brogath told himself. He decided it was time to pay a visit to an old friend – Lily, the kind girl who had cared for him when he first awoke in this strange world.

He found her tending to her garden, humming softly as she planted seeds for next season's harvest. When she saw Mr. Brogath approaching, her face lit up like a field of sunflowers.

"Mr. Brogath!" she exclaimed, wiping dirt-streaked hands on her apron. "What brings you here?"

"I wanted to thank you, Lily," he said sincerely, his eyes filled with gratitude. "When I first arrived in this world, lost and confused, you took care of me. I'll never forget your kindness."

Lily smiled warmly, touched by his words. "You're always welcome here, Mr. Brogath. We're all just trying to help each other in this world, aren't we?"

With a nod of agreement, Mr. Brogath bid Lily farewell and set off toward the castle, where Rila and Galen were busy planning the kingdom's future.

They had decided to dissolve the monarchy, believing that power should be shared among the people.

"Ah, Mr. Brogath," Rila greeted him with a firm handshake, her eyes sparkling with determination. "Glad you could join us."

"Rila, Galen," Mr. Brogath said, nodding to both of them. "I wanted to wish you the best in your endeavors. It's inspiring to see how far you've come and how you're working to create a better future for everyone."

"Thank you, Mr. Brogath," Galen replied, his voice steady and resolute. "We couldn't have done it without your help. We'll always be grateful for your guidance."

As they exchanged words of encouragement and camaraderie, Mr. Brogath couldn't help but feel a sense of contentment deep within his heart. Though uncertainty still lingered in the periphery of his thoughts, these connections he had forged – with Lily, Rila, Galen, and countless others – anchored him to the present.

After bidding Rila and Galen farewell, Mr. Brogath navigated the bustling city streets as a warm breeze carried the scent of fresh bread from a nearby bakery. The once-crumbling buildings now stood tall and proud, their vibrant colors a testament to the kingdom's renewed sense of hope.

He finally arrived at Roth's residence, a modest stone

house nestled in a quiet corner of the city. The door creaked open to reveal Roth standing in the doorway, his face brightening at the sight of Mr. Brogath.

"Ah, Mr. Brogath!" he exclaimed, clapping him on the back. "Come in, come in! You must be exhausted from your travels."

"Thank you, Roth," Mr. Brogath said, stepping into the cozy home that was filled with the soft glow of magical lights. He marveled at the transformation of the once-feared wizard, who now lived peacefully among the people he had protected for so long.

"Roth, I wanted to wish you well in your new life here," Mr. Brogath expressed, his eyes glistening with sincerity. "You've been through so much, and it's heartening to see you find solace and acceptance at last."

"Thank you, my friend," Roth replied, his voice tinged with gratitude. "I owe so much of this to you, as do the other wizards. Your unwavering belief in me helped me see that there was more to life than hiding in the shadows."

As they shared stories of their recent experiences, Mr. Brogath felt a profound connection with Roth — two lost souls seeking purpose in an ever-changing world. Their laughter echoed throughout the room, the weight of their pasts momentarily lifted. He told Mr. Brogath about how the now former king spent his days writing words of warning to any future would-be tyrants, using his own misguided life as an example. A fitting way to make amends.

"Roth, I've decided to stay in the kingdom for a while," Mr. Brogath confided, his gaze steady and resolute. "I want to help rebuild this place and, perhaps in doing so, find a piece of myself that's still missing. Though, I find myself caring less and less about my distant past with each passing day."

"Ah, Mr. Brogath," Roth said with a knowing nod. "I think you'll find that there's no better way to discover one's true self than by helping others. I wish you the best in your journey."

With heartfelt goodbyes, Mr. Brogath left Roth's home and ventured back into the sun-drenched streets. As he walked, he couldn't help but feel a growing sense of purpose.

He found himself among the workers rebuilding a once-grand library, its walls now scarred with cracks and crumbling mortar. With determination, Mr. Brogath picked up a trowel and began applying fresh cement, each stroke reconnecting the fractured stones like pieces of a puzzle.

As he labored alongside the people he had come to care for, Mr. Brogath felt the warmth of camaraderie envelop him like a comforting blanket. The air buzzed with contagious energy, laughter, and newfound hope. And amid the clatter of hammers and the scrape of trowels, Mr. Brogath found solace in the chaos – a sense of belonging that filled the void within him, if only for a moment.

Sunlight glinted off the trowel's blade as it sliced through the air, casting a bright flicker across the newly cemented stones. Mr. Brogath paused in his work, wiping sweat from his brow with a fur-covered forearm. The day had been long, but the progress was tangible – hope and determination blossomed within him like a golden flower unfurling its petals.

"Mr. Brogath!" called a familiar voice, carried on a gust of wind that brought with it the scent of fresh earth and blooming flowers. "An admirer approaches!"

He glanced up to see The Bearded Fool sauntering towards him, appearing out of nowhere like a mirage in the dusty haze. His loincloth fluttered in the breeze, and his bushy beard seemed to defy gravity as it bobbed along in front of him.

"Ah, The Bearded Fool," Mr. Brogath muttered beneath his breath, bracing himself for the inevitable onslaught of nonsensical banter. "What brings you to this humble construction site?"

The enigmatic figure stopped before him, scratching at his tangled beard as he gazed up at the partially rebuilt library. "The Bearded Fool has been watching you, my furry friend. Your determination is admirable, your intentions pure. You've come a long way. Perhaps The Bearded Fool can be of some assistance."

"Assistance?" Mr. Brogath echoed, curiosity piqued despite his best efforts. He set down his trowel and turned to face the peculiar man fully. "What do you mean?"

"Your memories, dear raccoon. The Bearded Fool sees how they weigh upon you, like a heavy stone chained to your heart." He reached into the depths of his beard and pulled forth a small, gleaming object, holding it out to Mr. Brogath. "This trinket may hold the key to unlocking the secrets of your past."

Mr. Brogath hesitated, glancing from The Bearded Fool's earnest expression to the object in his outstretched hand. It was a small silver key, its surface etched with intricate runes that seemed to shimmer and dance beneath the sun's rays. He felt a strange pull towards it, as if the key were calling out to something deep within him.

"Take it, Mr. Brogath," The Bearded Fool urged, sensing his indecision. "Embrace what it may reveal and let go of the fear that holds you back."

As Mr. Brogath's paw closed around the cool metal, a surge of emotion welled up within him – hope and trepidation mingling like oil and water. What would he discover when he unlocked the door this key belonged to? And more importantly, could he face whatever lay beyond it?

"Thank you," he whispered, the words barely audible amid the din of construction. "I don't know what I'll find, but perhaps it will lead me closer to understanding who I truly am. However, I'll be honest with you. I'm not sure I even want to know anymore."

A cryptic smile tugged at the corners of The Bearded Fool's mouth as he nodded. "Remember, Mr. Brogath," he said, stepping back. "Sometimes the greatest truths can be found by walking through the most unexpected doors."

Mr. Brogath clutched the silver key tightly in his paw, feeling its intricate runes pressing against his fur as he stared at The Bearded Fool. His heart raced with a mixture of fear and excitement - an odd combination that left him feeling more confused than anything else.

"Wait," Mr. Brogath said as he tried to process the cryptic words that had been spoken. "You're telling me that this key will help me regain my memories? But how? Where's the door?"

The Bearded Fool chuckled softly, the sound like a rustling of leaves on a crisp autumn day. "Ah, Mr. Brogath, always seeking answers without first asking the right questions."

"Then what is the right question?" Mr. Brogath asked, his brow furrowing in frustration. He thought of all the people he had encountered on his journey - Lily, Rila, Galen, Roth - and acknowledged that the present was also something worthy.

"Perhaps the better question is why you wish to regain your memories," The Bearded Fool replied, his eyes twinkling with mischief. "After all, sometimes it is our past that holds us back from embracing our future."

"I've always had the feeling that I was simply passing through, but also that I don't necessarily need to know who I am," Mr. Brogath insisted. "Yet, how can I move forward without understanding where I've come from?"

"Ah, therein lies the rub," The Bearded Fool mused, stroking his beard thoughtfully. "But perhaps the answer lies not in the past, but in the 'next world,' as it were."

"Next world?" Mr. Brogath echoed, his ears perking up at the mention of something unknown. His curiosity was piqued, and he couldn't help but wonder what new revelations awaited him there.

"Indeed," The Bearded Fool confirmed with a nod. "A place where the lines between reality and illusion blur, where truth and falsehood intertwine like the roots of an ancient tree, and where men of flesh fight men of metal."

"Sounds... confusing," Mr. Brogath admitted, his tail twitching in uncertainty.

"Confusing, yes, but also enlightening," The Bearded Fool replied, his voice taking on a reverent tone. "It is a realm that few have ventured into willingly, yet many have found themselves lost within its depths."

"Is it dangerous?" Mr. Brogath asked, his paw tightening around the key as he considered the implications of venturing into such a place.

"Only to those who are unprepared or unwilling to face the truths hidden within," The Bearded Fool answered cryptically. "But for one such as yourself, Mr. Brogath, I believe it may hold some of the answers you seek." He cackled, reconsidering his words. "Or maybe not. It's not like I can see into the future."

For a moment, Mr. Brogath stood there, weighing the risks and pondering the mysteries that lay ahead. As the sun dipped below the horizon, casting the world in twilight's embrace, he knew that he had come too far to turn back now.

"Alright," he said at last, his voice steady and determined. "I'll go to this 'next world' and see what awaits me there. But I won't forget the friends I've made here, nor the lessons I've learned."

"Oh, I wouldn't be too sure about that," The Bearded Fool said with a satisfied smile. "Remember, Mr. Brogath, sometimes doors can be passed through just by deciding you want to pass through them."

As the shadows crept across the cobblestones, Mr. Brogath took a deep breath, steeling himself.

The wind picked up, rustling the leaves overhead and ruffling Mr. Brogath's fur as he stared at The Bearded Fool. He felt the weight of his decision, like a stone heavy in his gut, as he considered the risks and benefits of accepting the mysterious offer. Memories tugged at him from beyond his reach, tantalizingly close but maddeningly elusive. Was it worth the uncertainty to find himself? To understand who he truly was?

"Is traveling between these worlds my purpose?" Mr. Brogath asked, his voice wavering slightly.

"How should I know? Perhaps," The Bearded Fool replied with an enigmatic smile. "But life is not without its uncertainties, Mr. Brogath. There are no guarantees."

Mr. Brogath's paw clenched and unclenched, his thoughts racing. He thought of the friends he'd made here in this world. They had helped shape the person he had become, even if he did not fully understand who that was yet. Could he risk leaving them behind, perhaps never to return?

"Are you sure you wish to embark on this journey alone?" The Bearded Fool prodded gently, as if sensing Mr.

Brogath's inner turmoil. "You have forged bonds with those around you. They may be able to help you bear the weight of your decision."

"Maybe," Mr. Brogath murmured, his eyes distant. "But this is my burden to bear, my path to walk. This is their world, but it isn't mine." He recalled Roth, standing tall and resolute in the face of adversity, and found himself inspired. "I must face whatever lies ahead on my own terms."

"Very well," The Bearded Fool said, nodding solemnly. "Remember, however, that the choice is always yours, and the door remains open."

As the sun dipped below the horizon, casting long shadows that stretched across the landscape, Mr. Brogath took a deep breath and squared his shoulders. The wind whipped around him, as if urging him forward. He knew he couldn't ignore the pull of another exciting journey any longer.

"I'll go," Mr. Brogath said.

"Then let your journey begin, Mr. Brogath," The Bearded Fool whispered, his eyes twinkling with an unspoken knowledge. "May you find something of value at your destination."

In the growing twilight, Mr. Brogath's footsteps echoed softly on the cobblestone streets as he walked away from The Bearded Fool. His heart felt heavy, yet strangely light at the same time, as if an unseen force had lifted an invisible burden from his shoulders. He could see the faces of Lily, Rila, Galen, and Roth in his mind's eye, their smiles warm and comforting, even though they couldn't be there with him now.

"Sometimes," he murmured to himself, "the hardest choices are the ones we make for ourselves, not for others."

A gentle breeze rustled the leaves above his head,

carrying the faint scent of wildflowers and fresh earth. It seemed as if the world itself was whispering its agreement, reminding him that even in the darkest times, hope persisted, blooming like a resilient flower amidst the rubble of despair.

"Even when we're lost," Mr. Brogath whispered to the wind, "we can still forge our own paths, discover who we truly are, and find our way back home."

As the stars began to emerge in the night sky, he gazed up, feeling a connection to something greater than himself. He realized that although his journey had been filled with trials and tribulations, each step had brought him closer to understanding the person he once was and the one he now wanted to become.

"No matter how far we stray from our beginnings, no matter how much we lose along the way, there is always a chance to reclaim what's ours and forge a brighter future," Mr. Brogath thought, a sense of peace washing over him.

With a newfound determination, he took one final look back at the city that had given him so much – friendship, love, and the hope of redemption – before turning towards the horizon and the unknown adventures that awaited him. He strode forward into the night, filled with the knowledge that even in the most uncertain times, there was always a flicker of hope to guide him on his journey.

EPILOGUE

Gears and bolts crunched under Mr. Brogath's paws as he stepped down from the mound of broken machines, his senses reeling in the metallic cacophony. He shook his head, trying to clear the fog that clouded his thoughts, but it stubbornly persisted.

"Where am I?" he muttered aloud, his voice sounding alien even to himself. His surroundings were nothing like the forest he had journeyed through before. Here, twisted metal and shattered glass littered the ground, the remnants of a once-advanced civilization.

"Who am I?" The question slipped from his lips unbidden, and it sent a shiver down his spine. Panic rose within him as he realized he couldn't remember anything about his past - not even the events leading up to this moment. It was as if he had been born anew atop that pile of discarded machinery.

"Alright, Mr. Brogath," he said, his voice quavering, "it seems you have some self-discovery to do."

He hesitated a moment, surprised at his own words. Mr. Brogath? Was that his name? It felt familiar, like a forgotten dream, but the more he tried to grasp it, the more it seemed to slip away.

"Focus," he chastised himself, forcing his attention back to his surroundings. Though he couldn't remember specific faces or names, a sense of camaraderie welled up within him, the ghost of bonds forged in his past. Those connections, however tenuous, gave him the strength to continue.

"Maybe someone around here can help me," he thought, scanning the desolate landscape for signs of life. But all he found were the decaying husks of buildings and the relentless wind that whipped across the barren plains, scattering debris in its wake.

"Or maybe not," he sighed, frustration gnawing at him. But he refused to let despair take hold. As disorienting as this new world was, Mr. Brogath couldn't shake the feeling that something here held the key to unlocking his lost memories.

"Alright then," he squared his shoulders, determination steeling his resolve, "let's see what you've got, strange new world."

With renewed purpose, Mr. Brogath ventured further into the desolation, driven by the mysteries surrounding his own identity and the instincts that had guided him throughout his previous journey. Amidst the wreckage of a forgotten civilization, he pressed on, ready to face whatever challenges lay ahead in his never-ending pursuit of adventure and self-discovery.

THANK YOU!

You made it to the end of the story. Nice! I really hope you enjoyed it.

If you have a couple of minutes to spare, please consider leaving a review! Reviews, especially written ones, are the literal lifeblood of any book series. Without reviews, new readers are unable to discover these books at all. If this was a story you enjoyed, I hope you'll help others to find it and enjoy it as well.

And okay, I'll admit... it feels really good to read nice reviews too. It's a big morale boost that keeps me motivated to write.

If you'd like to know when I publish a new book, you can follow me on the site where you purchased, but it's much more reliable to sign up for my newsletter (mrbrogath. com/newsletter). Plus, you can't beat the freebies, and they're exclusive to the mailing list! More on that later. Also, once upon a time I worked in marketing... so I hate it. I will never spam you to meet some kind of email quota. Cool announcements only.

Don't forget that I also have a Patreon (patreon.com/

mrbrogath), where members can get chapters well in advance for as little as $5 per month. I'll go over more of the perks later!

Thank you once again for your support. Without you, none of this would be possible. I am forever grateful.

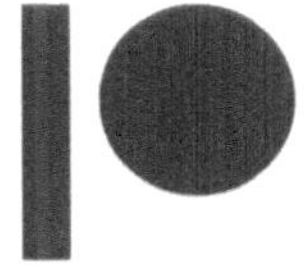

Members can, in addition to my bottomless gratitude, receive lots of cool perks by becoming a patron. Memberships start at as little as $3 a month, and it's one of the best ways to support me as an indie light novel author! These are just a few of the things you can get by joining:

- Early chapters for everything I write.
- Advanced review copies of my books.
- Exclusive artwork.

To sign up, visit my Patreon page here:
patreon.com/mrbrogath

Did you know I write other stuff too? Once upon a time, I kept all my series under different pen names, basically secret from one another. I've decided that I'll no longer do that, because I want to provide every reader with as much new content as possible! Even if you won't love everything I write, give it a look. You may be surprised and discover a new taste.

I THINK MY WRITING TUTOR HAS RABIES
LESSON 1:
THE FUNDAMENTALS
Mr. Brogath

A Kiss of Light and Flame
MR. BROGATH & M. OWENS

DETECTIVE
TRIGGER
AND THE RUBY COLLAR
MR. BROGATH AND M.A. OWENS

PANTECH CHRONICLES
SHADOWFALCON
BOOK I
F. LOCKHAVEN
M.A. OWENS

FREE STARTER PACK

Sign up for my mailing list to receive my free fiction starter pack, including:

- Mister Big (Detective Trigger)
- What's the Deal with Mailing Lists? (I Think My Writing Tutor Has Rabies)
- Nethalos Traveler's Guide (Tales of Love and Magic)
- PanTech Wallpaper Pack (PanTech Chronicles)

Get your freebies here:
mrbrogath.com/free

HOW TO FOLLOW

- Website (mrbrogath.com)
- Newsletter (mrbrogath.com/newsletter)
- Twitter (twitter.com/mrbrogath)
- Goodreads (goodreads.com/mrbrogath)
- Email (info@mrbrogath.com)
- YouTube (youtube.com/@mrbrogathacademy)
- Twitch (twitch.tv/mrbrogath)

www.ingramcontent.com/pod-product-compliance
Lightning Source LLC
Chambersburg PA
CBHW030755200726
48288CB00004B/1188